THE RASHERHOUSE

THE RASHERHOUSE

Alan Roberts

THE COLLINS PRESS

Published by The Collins Press, Careys Lane, The Huguenot
Quarter, Cork 1997

Printed in Ireland by Colour Books Ltd., Dublin

Jacket design by Upper Case Ltd., Cornmarket Street, Cork

ISBN: 1-898256-21-7

For my brother,
Don

Dᴇᴀʀ Rᴇᴀᴅᴇʀ. Nobody should be asked to read a book such as this! It is, to be frank, abominable. The style (if the writing can be dignified with such a description) indicates a narrow mind which has not developed beyond the adolescent stage. The language is appalling: every second word is an expletive, a sure indication of a sadly limited vocabulary. I have sanitised the text where possible to protect the reader from the worst excesses, but I am forced to leave in a lot of the filth, in order to convey the ambiance.

With regard to the spelling and the grammar, again I have done my best to render an almost unreadable text legible, while at the same time ensuring that I kept as much of the original phonetics as is necessary to maintain the atmosphere of the story.

The very name, *The Rasherhouse*, forewarns us of the prurience to come. Male prisoners refer to the women's prison in Mountjoy as 'The Rasherhouse', 'rasher' being a male prisoner's euphemism for sexual intercourse.

We do not live in an ideal world, so there is a purpose in being aware of this type of writing.

Sadly, in this age of television and video, readers of books tend to be from the higher socio-economic groupings only. As a result, I feel justified in bringing the attention of readers to this text, even though it borders on the pornographic. If, however, any of my readers are among those sad voyeuristic individuals who might be looking for vicarious thrills, I must advise them now that this book will be of no interest to them whatsoever. I have brought my editorial skills to bear not only on grammar and spelling but more importantly in the sphere of morality. Several passages which obviously were inserted for the sole purpose of titillation, I have omitted. To the genuine reader, interested in sociology, crime and punishment, I must warn that the text still contains harrowing passages, which I could not omit without doing an injustice to my case.

Let me introduce myself and explain my purpose. I am Seán Howard, a retired senior civil servant from the

Department of Justice. Having joined the Department on leaving school, I rose through the ranks at a very satisfactory rate and, while still a young man, became a higher clerical officer. This position carries a good measure of responsibility and, because of my dedication to my work, I was honoured to have been asked regularly to advise various Ministers for Justice on matters relating to prisons. Indeed, many a ministerial speech on crime and punishment owed more than a little to my work. I can say without fear of contradiction that I became one of the country's leading experts in criminology and that prison regimes throughout the land showed signs of my influence, much to the enhancement of their smooth and efficient running.

Prisons attract the attention of all sorts of 'do gooder' groups; they have done so since the time of the French Revolution. A healthy democracy such as ours can and should listen to these well-meaning people, and on the rare occasions when their concerns are well-founded, suggestions they may have can be listened to with profit. I pride myself on having always been ready to give such groups a sympathetic ear.

In the late 1970s, however, a bevy of new groups (without experience or insight) insisted on making strident and unfounded accusations about the women's prison in Mountjoy. I had always taken a personal interest in this unit – it was the only women's prison in the state, and it had been given as my special brief. These concerned citizens are members of 'the feminist movement', although I must admit that I cannot see what is even vaguely feminine about their behaviour. The immediate cause of their 'concern' was an unfortunate series of incidents which took place in the women's prison. There were at that time, and to some extent there still are, minor problems relating to this unit. Ironically, the problems were exacerbated by the protests of these groups. The feminists loudly complained about conditions in the prison, which I hasten to add were satisfactory, as they had been for decades. Such complaints increased the

2

expectations of the inmates, which in turn raised their levels of dissatisfaction. The outcome was a series of disturbances and a small riot. Several prisoners attempted suicide around this time.

I reacted as any public servant should in the circumstances: I maintained a steady course and was not influenced by these unenlightened and disruptive elements. None of the well-heeled members of the chattering classes who involved themselves had ever been inside a prison, having more personal ambition than social concern. Their idea seemed to be that women prisoners were more sinned against than sinning and that, as a result, the women's prison should resemble a first-class hotel.

By the middle of the 1980s, some of these women achieved the positions of power to which they had so obviously aspired. Most of them conveniently forgot the women's prison and the other causes which they had used to gain public attention for themselves. One or two doggedly pursued their ill-conceived campaign. In time I found myself at the receiving end of criticisms and even abuse, which, because of my position as a senior civil servant, I was not allowed to rebut. More seriously, I was rapidly finding myself in a situation where I either had to be involved in rewarding criminals with conditions better than they had experienced before imprisonment or leave the position of responsibility that I had worked a lifetime to achieve. I opted for early retirement, although I was still in my fifties.

Now, having gained my independence and the freedom to refute the accusations, I intend to put the record straight. Drawing on a lifetime's experience in prison reform, I wish to show how these pressure groups are doing a huge disservice to society.

To facilitate this, I will use this typescript. Never before has a piece of literary drivel been put to such good use, albeit the opposite use to which it was intended.

Fortuitously, the text came into my hands towards the (premature) end of my career in the Department. If I had to describe it, I would say that it is a seriously misguided attempt at social realism, a crude and ugly effort at what is called 'agitprop' in the world of drama, a work in which political propaganda takes precedence over aesthetics.

Written by an inmate of the women's prison, a woman with a history of serious offending, it was confiscated during a routine cell search, submitted to the Department and eventually to myself, to assess if it served any purpose other than as a mischievous attack on the prison system. My decision, not that it would have been a hard one, was rendered unnecessary by the subsequent death of the author as a result of AIDS-related illnesses. Now having edited and sanitised it somewhat, I will use it to illustrate the poverty of the case for prison reform.

In literary terms, what I want to do is to deconstruct the text. By that I mean that I intend to subject it to a particular method of criticism and of analytical inquiry. I will, every now and then, undo the text and expose the opposing forces within it to show that it is saying something quite different to what it appears to be saying. By bringing the reader's attention to underlying layers of meaning, I will make the work betray itself as a rather clever but ultimately shallow piece of propaganda, written by a writer full of thinly-disguised hate for all that is decent in society. I will peel away layers of meaning, not to expose the one true meaning, for no text has such, but to expose the author's mischievous intentions – intentions which sadly bear fruit when such work reaches readers like my critics, who, for the want of a genuine understanding of the issues, see in its surface meaning the only authentic reflection of reality.

Before I start, perhaps it would be best to give you, Dear Reader, a taste of the offending document.

Mags sat on the courtroom bench beside her solicitor, her baby asleep in her arms. Instinct told her to look as tough as her plump, five foot two inches would allow, but the solicitor had advised her to bring the baby and to appear 'vulnerable'. She could not even guess the meaning of the word, and so she just sat and kept the baby as quiet as possible for the two hours while she waited for her case to be heard. When her turn came, the complete proceedings had taken only two minutes and now the judge was scrutinising her as he spoke.

'Bla bla bringing babies into court bla not impressed bla bla second time bla seventeen is old enough to know what you are doing bla bla ...' Mags stared back into the judge's face, fascinated by his wrinkled skin and huge purple nose, his head draped in the stupid wig thing. Desperately trying to understand what he was saying, she was able to make out only the occasional word.

'Bla bla congratulate your defending counsel bla environmental factors bla bla jurisprudential concepts bla individual free choice bla bla bla.'

Something in his voice gave her the jitters. She was scared to even be in court, but everyone, even her solicitor, said she would again get away with a warning. A few more words were beginning to make sense to her and she did not like the sound of them or the tone of old purple nose's voice.

'Bla bla learn your lesson bla held in custody bla six months bla bla prison.'

She turned to her solicitor, who did not look any older than herself.

'Wha' did he say?'

'I'm sorry, Margaret, but you are going to prison for six months.' Red showed over his white starched collar, rising to his spoilt schoolboy's face.

'Wha'?'

'The judge has sentenced you to six months' detention in Mountjoy Women's Prison, Margaret.'

'Don't be bleedin' stupa'! Sure how could I look after the baby in prison, in the name a Jasus?'

'You won't be able to, Margaret. You'll have to find someone to look after her for you, or she'll be taken into

5

care.'

Mags' voice was rising now and in the babble of voices between court cases it was heard above all the others.

'Come off it! She's only six months old, sure!'

The baby began to cry as the solicitor stood up, hurriedly arranging papers into his slim black briefcase. 'I'm sorry, Margaret, I did my best for you. We were very unlucky with the judge we got. As you know, I postponed the case twice, hoping we'd get another judge, but it can't be undone now. Would you like me to ask the court to make arrangements to have the baby taken into care?'

The next court case was already underway as Mags' reply rang around the room.

'Fuck you and the fuckin' court!'

The baby jumped with fright as the judge's gavel smashed onto the block; he threatened to have Mags taken to prison immediately if she did not leave the court quietly. A policeman propelled her out. Or was it a policewoman? Mags could see only a large figure through her tears. She squeezed her child to her as a huge hand clamped her upper arm and guided her to a small room swimming with blue uniforms.

By now Mags' anguish had been transmitted to her child, who was screaming. A pair of chubby arms enveloped the two heaving bodies.

'Don't cry, my little love, don't cry, please, love, for your Mammy. Please now, Mags, don't be so upset, be strong for your Mammy and for your little babby.'

Margaret's mother was even smaller than herself. Only four foot eleven inches, she commanded a presence which belied her size. She had her daughter's considerable beauty but in a much worn version. At thirty-five she was almost twice Mags' age. Her huge dark eyes were fighting to keep back the tears. Mags knew whose arms had encircled her before she heard the reassuring voice.

'Everything's going to be all right, little love, everything will be just fine. I'll look after baby Tracy till you get out.

Sure she will be as happy as Larry, an' I'll bring her up to see you every day, so I will. Sure everything will work out just fine, love. I won't let anyone be cruel to you or to little Tracy, honest love. Now stop your crying and give the baby her bottle.'

The bottle of juice was put to the baby's mouth and the convulsions eased as she sucked greedily on the plastic teat. Her big dark eyes were open and her eyebrows stayed arched, as if she had just seen a ghost.

'But, Ma, it was just a poxy two hundred pound worth a baby clothes.'

'I know, love, I know, but ya were warned the last time, remember? We all told ya that if ya were caught again this would happen. Didn't we, love? I told ya that if ya needed anything for Tracy, I had a couple of shilling put aside in the Credit Union, didn't I?'

Now it was Mrs O'Brien's turn to break down. Her big, tear-filled eyes overflowed and brought long black lines of mascara down her handsome face.

'Now, ladies, it's not the end of the world. Come on, this will make ye feel better now. Would ye like some biscuits?' The big policewoman had an air of much-tried patience as she gave them cups of tea. The cups rattled on their saucers as the women took the hot sugary brew.

'Look, Margaret, it's not as bad as it seems. We're not going to bring you in today. We'll send an unmarked car to your house on Monday morning. That'll give you lots of time to make any arrangements that you want and the neighbours need know nothing about it at all. And as well, Margaret, you won't do anything like the six months. With good behaviour, sure you'll be out in four. Now, come on, drink up your tea and ye can be off whenever you want.'

The Ban Garda's windswept face swopped its look of tolerance for one of menace with the rapidity of a professional actor.

'Make sure you're at your place at ten on Monday morning though, won't you, Margaret?'

Dear Reader. I'm sure that you can see the general tone emerging already. The 'woe is me' attitude so common among those segments of society who feel that the world owes them a living. We are supposed to feel sorry for the single mother and excuse her any crime against society because she lacked the moral fibre to control, or at least regulate, her own desires.

Lest I am attacked by genuinely concerned women (as opposed to the fanatics of the radical wing of the feminist movement), let me say immediately that statistics prove that women in general are highly trustworthy and law-abiding. Constituting, as they do, fifty percent of the population, women account for only two percent of crime, and their share of violent crime is a minute fraction of that figure. Women offenders are, however, a growing proportion of prison inmates and I can't help wondering if this is not in some way due to the excesses of radical feminist propaganda, which encourages aggression among women. Previously the criminal fraternity was totally opposed to their women partaking in crime, this being against their machismo self-image. Now, with women being coerced out of their time-honoured role as carers, they are being pushed into single motherhood, drugs into crime in rising numbers. So much for the joys of women's liberation!

The judge in the typescript was implicitly ridiculed for using terms such as 'individual free choice'. How sad the author's attitudes must have been, accepting, as she appears to have, the discredited philosophy of determinism, which holds that we have no free will but that all our actions are merely uncontrollable reactions to earlier stimuli. What a convenient position for the lazy, lustful and immoral to hold, claiming as they do that they are conditioned by their environment and are not responsible for any action whatsoever? If we are to accept that criminals are determined by their environment to commit crime, then we might as well abandon the criminal justice system. Hitler would be seen as a blameless victim of his environment and so one to be pitied for his actions, over which he had no control.

All I can say to such arrant nonsense is that my sympathy would lie with the judge when he sent the young girl to prison to learn a thing or two. The offender did indeed make individual free choices, for which the judge was absolutely correct to punish her.

Typically, 'the prison as luxury hotel' lobby subscribe to this determinism nonsense and have thereby caused more than a small amount of harm to our custodial institutions!

Never had time gone so fast as between her sentencing and incarceration. The two girls with whom Mags had become friendly since moving out to Clondalkin called on her each night to go for a couple of pints. Having gone to great trouble to find baby-sitters for their own kids, Mags, to their great annoyance, would not leave Tracy, so they stayed in her place with a few cans and watched videos.

Baby-sitters were just about impossible to find on the estate. All her neighbours seemed to be about Mags' age and to have a few kids. But lack of a baby-sitter was not the problem. She had not let Tracy out of her sight in the six months since the baby had been born and she was certainly not going to now.

The girls tried their best to cheer her up.

'Jasus, ya should go to the local an' get yourself one a dem rides that come out here at the weekends. It will be your last chance for a while for a bit of the other.'

As much as she appreciated their trying, she could not even pretend to laugh at that suggestion.

'Bollix to the randy bastards.'

Sunday was a nightmare. She scrubbed the little house from top to bottom for the umpteenth time, packed a Dunnes Stores plastic bag with what she thought she might need in prison, made sure every stitch of Tracy's clothes were washed and ironed, then brought the child out in her buggy for a long walk. She discovered parts of the estate she

9

had never known existed.

When she got home, her mother would be there to take the baby to her flat in town. She was walking to postpone that moment, to exhaust herself in the hope of getting to sleep that night and blocking out the pain.

Row after row of identical Legoland houses made Mags more dizzy than tired. She thought of all the terrible television programmes about prisons she had seen, and she shivered. But the prospect of parting with Tracy – her reason for living – was what really terrified her.

In the six months since the baby had been born, she had known happiness for the first time. Being needed had given her a reason to live. She thought of her mother, whom she really loved too, but that was different. Her ma had her fella, fucker that he was, and that had put a barrier between mother and daughter.

Blue flickering light shone from the miniature front rooms of the cloned houses. The roars of a football crowd exploded at intervals through the windows into the grey plastic-strewn road. From one or two front rooms, an adult male voice led the tirade of abuse. Rusty trikes and huge broken dolls' prams lay abandoned in mucky gardens. A disgruntled gnome surveyed a thriving crop of dandelions growing from cracks in the patch of concrete which held him captive. Graffiti competed for space on garden walls.

Among dozens of other scrawled, misspelt messages, the words, 'Tracy is a cunt' jumped out at Mags. The sprayed words hit her like a slap in the face. The rest of the graffiti was just ugly undecipherable hieroglyphics, since she was able to read only her own name, Tracy's and about ten other words. She could read 'love', 'hate', 'sex', 'fuck', 'cunt' and 'bollix'. The only sentences she could recognise were, 'Paddy loves Mary,' and 'Mary is a cunt'. The names changed, of course, but these messages of love and hate were on every second wall and hoarding and constituted her complete literary education.

'What bastard writ that?' she wanted to shout. Seeing

her little baby's name among the filth made her feel sick. She wanted to tear down the wall.

A grey mist was starting to wet her clothes. Pulling the cover over Tracy's blankets, she zipped up her shiny tracksuit and hurried on.

She turned a corner and found herself on a huge main road. Although she could see for a long way up and down, there was not a car in sight – just the empty dual carriageway disappearing into the grey distance. Plastic bags littered the road, even more than in the estate, and on the far side were huge mounds of muck. There was a track between two of the piles. Maybe the path led to a little wood with a lake, like you'd see in the ads for shampoo, Mags thought. She crossed the dual carriageway after a single car sped past.

It was difficult to push the pram through the mud, but she persisted. Sinking deep into slime, her runners soaked up water, but the grass looked drier and she pushed on.

The 'grass' turned out to be a tangle of nettles and prickly thorns, but it was firmer underfoot and she pushed the pram through it. There was no comic-book woods and lake with graceful swans. As far as Mags could see through the fog, weeds did deadly battle for supremacy with broken cars, abandoned fridges and washing machines. Giant thistles grew out of the eye sockets of rotting machines.

'Fuck this!' she said and turned around to get back home.

When she saw them, she nearly had a fit.

There must have been about ten of them, all teenage fellas, sitting around a big fire of old tyres and plastic milk crates which spewed black clouds of toxic fumes into the sky. They were swilling cider from huge plastic bottles. How she had not observed them on the way in to the wasteland she did not know, but she saw them clearly now. She could see the tattoos, the scarred cheek of the big blonde guy, the grey scalps of the shaven-headed ones, the leers on the faces.

Instinct took over and she mastered her impulse to try and rush back to the road. The look of innocence on her face was transformed by a new look in her eyes which falsely spoke of belligerence.

'Here missus.' A bottle was held out by a guy of about fourteen. 'Ja want a sup?'

'Bit early for me.' Mags' voice conveyed a mixture of boredom and confidence. Just enough of the former so as not to encourage the gang; enough of the latter not to let them sense her fear.

'Here, come on over. Ya can have my seat so ya can.' Slurring, the scarred one indicated the upturned plastic bucket. 'Come on, we've plenty to go round.'

He held up his bottle as he staggered towards the gap Mags was making for.

'We'll look after the snapper while ya have a good time,' slurred another and a snigger went around the gang.

She tried to force the buggy through the mud without giving the impression that she was afraid, but as Scarface got near to her escape route, her heart began to pound. He stopped in front of her and she could see that his eyes were glazing, his leer exposing broken and discoloured teeth.

'Sure ya shouldn't ask a lady to sit on a bucka, for Jasus' sake,' shouted one of the gang. 'I'd give her sometin' a lot bleedin' hotter to sit on, so I would.'

The speaker stood, rubbing his groin and contorting his face into a look of pained ecstasy.

The laughter was cut short by Mags' shout as she stabbed a finger towards him.

'I know where you live, ya little scumbag ya. If I tell me husband what you just said, ya dead! Ya hear me, do ya?'

The dirty, fire-reddened faces turned to their mate. He hesitated.

'Was only bleedin' joking for fuck's sake.'

'Yea, well never joke like that with me again, ri'?'

Mags pushed the buggy towards the gap as wails of distress erupted from the baby.

'Get outa me fuckin' way you!'

The scarred one held his ground, but his smirk

disappeared and, as the buggy was about to hit him, he stepped aside.

As Mags tried to walk nonchalantly back to the comparative safety of the houses, a roar of laughter broke out. Half-a-dozen drunken voices drowned her baby's cries.

'Poxy cunt!' Mags heard. 'Ugly scumbag!'

Tears ran down her cheeks as she hurried down the first side road she came to.

When her tears stopped and she looked around, she was lost in a maze of concrete houses. Hurrying on, she began to recognise some features: the travellers' house with the broken down cars, the burnt-out house and, near home, the patch of grass used as a dump. There were kids out on the street now and she knew some of the pale little faces.

'Ay missus, an awl one's after goin' into ya gaff.'

Relief at being safely home vanished. Her mother had come to take Tracy away. The black depression which had given way to fear slammed back into place. A deep urge to run came over Mags, but she knew there was nowhere to hide. She opened the door reluctantly.

'Mags, love.' Her mother's voice was full of concern. 'Look at ya, you're soaking. Ya shouldn't have the child out in that awl mist, so ya shouldn't; bad for her little chest, and yours. You're as pale as a sheet.'

'I'm OK, Ma.'

But her mother's face showed no sign of reassurance; she looked old before her time. The scar under her left eye was purple against her pale skin. 'Look, you go and get out a that damp tracksuit and I'll change Tracy.' She was making a superhuman effort to sound cheerful.

Mags was beyond pretence.

'No, Ma, I'll change her meself. You go and put the kettle on.'

Lifting the baby out of the buggy, Mags carried her upstairs where she collapsed on the bed and, hugging the child to her heaving breast, silently cried.

She was still sobbing ten minutes later when her mother came up.

'Now, now, me little angel, there's nothing to cry about. She'll be happy with me. Sure your baby brother will be good company for her. They'll have great times together, honest love. Ya know that love, don't ya?'

Now both women were crying. Mags put her arms out and gently pulled her mother towards her; their bodies rose and fell in unison as sobs enveloped them. Nestled between the two women, the baby made the gentlest sound of protest. Looking down and seeing her wide-eyed in an expression of bewilderment, they burst out laughing. Mags lifted the child towards the ceiling.

'You, ya little divil ya, I can see ya going to be spoilt rotten in the next couple a months, so I can.'

Sleep eluded Mags that night. After her mother had left with Tracy, Mags drank a naggin of vodka, but she was unaccustomed to drinking spirits, and all it did was add to her anxiety.

Getting up early, she cleaned the house yet again. She found a packet of cigarettes which her mother had forgotten, and smoked her first since before Tracy's birth.

The two policemen called at ten. Culchies, of course! Big and strong, they looked as if they ate too much. And yet they were not really fat. Sitting in the back of the car, she discovered how the name red-neck had come about. They were from a different world than the guys she knew. She reckoned they were speaking Irish because she could understand only an occasional word. As they laughed and joked during the journey, as if Mags was not in the car, she felt like a piece of meat being transported to a factory.

As promised, the car had no markings, but Mags felt sure that everyone was gawking at her as they drove through the estate. If only she could get them to stop the car and let her go to her mammy and the baby! 'Two months off for good behaviour', the solicitor had said. She would act tough to survive, but she would be a model prisoner. She would give them nothing to complain about, and be out in four months and not a day longer.

Because she was so nervous, before long, Mags was dying to go to the toilet. Jasus, what would she do if she couldn't hold on?

The car swung into a narrow laneway and there it was. There was no mistaking it. What else could those huge grey walls be? The gates were like the gates of Hell. As the car stopped and her door was opened, her resolve not to show weakness deserted her. Standing out, her legs shook and she thought she was going to collapse.

'First time, hah?'

A glimmer of humanity flickered in the policeman's eyes, but Mags was afraid that if she opened her mouth she would burst out crying. Getting no reply, the country-fresh face settled back into cold detachment.

He rang a bell. A peep-hole crashed open with the sound of a hammer hitting cast iron. Eyes peered through the small barred opening, lingered on Mags for a second and then the spy-hole crashed shut again. More hammer on metal sounds followed as a door within the gates opened into a large barred cage. Mags was rooted to the spot. Thoughts of running flashed through her terror-stricken mind, but it was all she could do to stay standing.

Her plastic bag of belongings was handed in, along with her particulars on a piece of paper. A large hand, bred for pushing a plough, propelled Mags firmly through the opening and she was in prison.

The door slammed shut with an ear-piercing crash.

The gate-man handed her back her plastic bag and scanned the piece of paper.

'Sit down there now, you poor little thing.' He indicated a bench. The kindly tone of voice put an end to Mags' attempt at looking tough. She burst out crying.

'Yerra now, Margaret. Sure there's no need of that now, so there's not. Sure it's not the end of the world you know.'

Mags wiped her eyes with her sleeve.

'That's better now. Sure do you know what? I get girls knocking on this door asking to be let in. I do, I do. Some of the women who have been in here prefer it to being out and about. Now isn't that hard to believe? There ya are now, there ya are.' He picked up a phone.

'Gate,' he said into the phone and resumed the speech as if he had made it a million times.

'Can't be all that bad, can it now, hah?'

His face was wrinkled into a permanent look of concern, with the eyes of a countryman who had seen too much of city life.

'Gate,' a woman's voice shouted. She was dressed in an ugly dark-blue uniform and was standing at the other side of the bars. Another officer appeared at her side and opened the gate with an enormous key. It was similar to one of the keys Mags had seen on eighteenth-birthday cards and it reminded her that she would be out in time for her own eighteenth birthday, and her ma would give her a card with a huge big key on it like that. She would go out with her for a good few jars and everything would be great again.

'Margaret O'Brien?'

'Yea.'

'Come along.'

The officer was a large, heavy countrywoman. She did not say a word as they walked across a big square, boxed in by long grey buildings with four rows of small barred windows, one over the other, in each. A few officers scurried about and a dozen young fellas dressed in grey jumpers and blue jeans were sweeping. Gaunt, pimply adolescents, their macho posturing on seeing the new girl being led across the yard only made them look pathetic.

'Ay, tits.'

Mags looked, with what she hoped was a look of defiance, at the group of sweepers, but they just stared back with broad green-toothed grins and nudged one another. The shout hadn't come from them. Maybe it hadn't been meant for her at all.

'Hey good-looking! You with the big tits an' the black hair.'

16

Mags could feel her face go bright red. Her breasts had never gone back to what they had been before she had given birth to Tracy. Much to her distress, they were bigger than her mother's and she was hyper-sensitive about them. Despite herself, she looked around but could not figure out where the shouting had come from.

'Up here, ya silly cunt ya.'

Mortified, she wanted the ground to open and swallow her up, but instinctively her head turned as she located the source of the shouts. At one of the barred and meshed windows she could just make out the top of a man's head. In the moment that her eyes lingered, she could see heads appear at every window. She faced forward and quickened her pace.

'What's ya name, big tits?'

Mags walked on in silence as a dozen voices spat a cacophony of obscenities down at her.

'Ja do oral, do ya?'

'Suppose a fuck's outa the question?'

'Hope you got a good ride last night, cos ya won't be gettin' it much where you're goin'.'

'Sept if ya inta fuckin' the dikes.'

'Are ya a lezzer, are ya but?'

'Here, ya can pretend this is a cucumber any time, so ya can.'

Like the audience at a strip show, the sweepers relished Mags' humiliation. She walked as closely behind the officer as possible, hoping she could hide in her shadow.

The officer rang a bell in an iron door. This was opened by another female officer and Mags was led up some steps, through another iron gate and into one of the buildings from where the shouting had been coming. She thought she was about to come face to face with her tormentors but, as she was to learn, the women's prison took up only the bottom two floors of this building. The top two floors and all the other buildings surrounding the yard were occupied by young male prisoners.

17

'Give me that and stand there.'

The officer took Mags' plastic bag and went into a small office. Reading from the piece of paper, she began to write into a large ledger.

Mags' bladder was about to burst. She went to the door of the office.

'Please, miss, I need to go to the toila.'

'You'll just have to wait now, Margaret.'

'Jasus, miss, I'm burstin' so I am, burstin'.'

'Huh, come with me then.'

At a small cubicle, the officer pointed to a metal toilet bowl. There was no door and Mags, now desperate, waited for her to leave.

'Come on,' the officer growled. 'I haven't all day.'

Mags was torn between the need to relieve herself and her natural modesty. A male officer passed by without looking their way.

'Jasus, I can't with you there.'

Leaning into the cubicle, the officer unhooked a minute swing door.

'Now hurry.' She stared at Mags, who, thighs clamped together, waddled into the cubicle.

The door left her almost totally exposed, but pressure on her bladder overcame all other considerations.

With relief came embarrassment. As the flow eased, without warning came the sound of a fart, amplified a hundred-fold by the metal. She had never been so mortified in all her life, not even when she was having the baby and they did all those horrible things to her. Pulling up her pants as quickly as she could, she rushed back to the spot where she had been told to stand, as the officer went back to writing.

Through tear-filled eyes, she started to take in her surroundings. She was in a large rectangular hall with a barred gate at either end and ten metal doors on each side. A metal staircase led up to a balcony, which was also lined with cells. The two landings were separated by a heavy wire mesh where a ceiling would normally have been.

The place looked dirty but then the grey walls made things look grubby. There was no natural light except that which came in the barred gates. Strip lights struggled to fill the darkness of the hall. An overpowering smell of disinfectant reminded Mags of the toilets in her old school.

She shivered, and wondered why. The hall was not cold. It must have been all the metal which made her feel strangely cold in the warmth. Everything she could see was either concrete or iron, cruelly hard and metallic.

A male officer came into the hall, slamming the gate shut. A beer-bellied old fella, he must have been forty at least, Mags reckoned. He had a fat country face on him like all the rest of the officers, but she had to admit that it was a kind face. Voices cackled from a walkie-talkie radio strapped to his waist as he sat on a chair halfway down the hall and began reading a tabloid newspaper.

'Read this,' the female officer handed her a form, 'and sign your name at the bottom.'

Mags became flustered.

'Sorry, miss, but I forgot to bring me glasses in with me an' I can't see a thing without 'em.'

The officer smiled sarcastically. 'Yes, a lot of girls "forget" to bring their glasses. Put an "X" where my finger is.'

Mags made an 'X' at the bottom of the paper.

'Now strip.'

'Wha'?'

'Strip.'

'Take me clothes off, ya mean?' She looked towards the male officer.

'That's right, Margaret.' With an exaggerated smile on her face, the officer stressed each word as if she were addressing an idiot. 'You can stand in there.'

She pointed to a shower-head near the toilet. It too was screened from view only by a minute swinging 'door'. Mags could feel her face go red again. She looked towards the male officer, then rushed into the cubicle, hoping to have this over before he might come up the hall.

'Now give yourself a good shower and then put these on.'

The officer took Mags' shiny tracksuit, searched the pockets, put everything into a black bag and left clean clothes on a chair.

After the quickest shower she had ever had, she pulled the clothes onto her wet body. They were like the ones she had seen the sweepers wearing on the way in. The jeans were great, but she felt she looked horrible in the grey woolly jumper.

'Ready for this one, Paddy?' the female officer shouted to the pot-bellied paper reader.

'Yes, Officer Rice, I am. Send her along.'

'Go down to that officer and give him this.' Mags was handed a small square of paper.

'Hello, young lady, and what would your name be now?' He spoke in a fatherly tone, wheezing slightly. She hoped this officer would be in charge of her, not the one called Rice.

'Mags, mister,' she stammered.

He scanned the piece of paper.

'Margaret, that's a lovely name. Now don't you worry about a thing, Margaret. Sure you'll be out of here and home again in no time, so you will now.'

'Thanks, mister.'

'You can call me Paddy; everyone else does. Now follow me, Margaret.'

Shuffling down the landing, he looked at the piece of paper again and his face took on an expression of annoyance. He led her to one of the heavy grey doors and unlocked it.

'Well, Margaret, this will be your home for the next few months.' He pushed the door open with an effort. 'God help you!' he murmured.

Not exactly Jane Austen, dear Reader, is it? It will, however, do nicely to illustrate some important points about the modern prison system. Reading the text from here on, I would ask you to bear in mind the contribution of Jeremy Bentham to the study of criminology, and in particular, his wonderful architectural idea, which he called the 'Panopticon'.

Bentham, whose philosophy could be summed up in the phrase 'let the punishment fit the crime', was born in 1748. He was one of the founding fathers of Liberalism, which is not a philosophy I have any regard for myself. However, I think his ideas on crime and punishment were very perceptive. They were self-evidently common sense and based on a shrewd understanding of human nature.

The Panopticon was Bentham's ingenious design for the ideal prison. Shaped like a wheel, it was a simple ring of prison cells, surrounding a smaller circle which could not be observed from this outer ring. In the inner circle were the prison guards. Since the guards had a perfect view of all the cells but could not themselves be seen, very few of them were needed. In the outer circle, each prisoner's every move could be monitored through their barred cells but they could not see or speak to each other. That each cell would accommodate only one prisoner, who would not be allowed to communicate with any other and who knew he was under constant surveillance, was essential to Bentham's design. Strict silence and lots of hard work would allow the inmates to dwell on their lives and to meditate on the wrong that they had done. The Panopticon was thus cheap to run and not a 'university of crime', as unfortunately modern-day prisons undoubtedly are. Bentham neatly expressed the purpose of the Panopticon as 'to grind rogues honest'.

Bentham thought that his design would prove suitable for use in other institutions, such as hospitals, factories and schools. Modern theories of personnel management or 'human resources management' as they call it today, would rightly reject such a God's eye level of observation. For the prison, however, then as now, Bentham's idea makes a great deal of sense. No Panopticon was ever built, but as the reader wades through more of the text below, he will begin to see the desirability of such a design.

A thick blue fog of smoke billowed out as the door opened and Mags was engulfed by the smell of tobacco, piss and smelly feet. It was all she could do not to gag.

'In you go now, love.' Paddy waved his arms around in the air.

Trembling, Mags stepped into the cramped space. Between the smoke, the dim light and her fear, it took her a few seconds to focus on her surroundings. She was in an area a little bigger than her own bathroom. The walls were either filthy or painted browny green. Two sets of bunk beds barely left enough space for a person to stand. Two metal bedside lockers, a tray-sized table and one bockety plastic chair completed the furnishings. The ceiling was domed and high. A dim light came from a strip tube embedded in the ceiling and a small, barred and meshed window high up in the wall facing the metal door.

'Howya, love, first time hah?'

The voice sounded genuinely concerned, but Mags was afraid to answer. She had expected to have a cell to herself and was horrified to find two women lying on the bottom bunks. She nodded timidly to her cell mates.

'Ahhh, God help ya, don't be upset but. Ya in for long?' one of the women asked.

'Six months,' she managed to answer before being convulsed by tears.

'Ah Jasus, sure that's only time for a shit an' a shower. Sure you'll be out in no time arall, honest ya will. Don't cry now. What's ya name hah?'

'Mags.'

'That's lovely, that is.' Smiling, she exposed a mouthful of multi-coloured teeth. 'Dey call me Betty.'

Betty spoke in a tired drawl, every word an effort. She

looked about thirty going on sixty, was skinny and looked small on the bunk. Her face, which once must have been very beautiful, Mags thought, was now a greeny-white with a long blue scar running from ear to chin. Grey lines circled eyes with most of their blue drained from them, grey hair hung lankly and turned pitch black two inches from the scalp – a face much abused by life but still loveable.

'I'm Rosie. Just in case ya want ta know like.'

Heavy sarcasm overlaid the voice from the other bunk. The woman there was about forty, big and fat. A lot less haggard-looking than Betty, Mags thought, but perhaps that was because she was so heavily made up. Dollops of mascara encircled small green eyes; her lips were plastered bright red. Her blonde hair looked brittle enough to shatter if touched.

Mags took the half step towards the big blonde's bunk and put out her hand.

'Pleased to meet ya, Rosie.'

'Oh, the feelin' is mutual, I'm sure.' Rosie mimicked a posh accent without taking the outstretched hand. Mags let her arm fall to her side and sat on the only chair in the cell. Betty handed her a half-smoked roll-up. 'Here love, have a drag. Make ya feel better.'

Drawing in heavily, Mags took a fit of coughing when the unfamiliar sensation hit her lungs.

'Jasus, we have a right one here!' Rosie boomed out. 'Don't tell me ya never smoked dope before?'

'Did so!' Mags did not sound convincing.

Betty sat up with sudden interest.

'Ay listen, what ja bring in with ya?'

'Change of clothes, soap, shampoo an' ...'

'Fuck shampoo an' soap. I mean gear.'

'Gear?'

'Ya know smack, dike, palf, naps, any fuckin' thing.'

'I'm not into any a that stuff. I have a baby to look after.'

Betty slumped back down on the bunk like a puppet whose strings had been cut. Mags started to cry again.

23

'Ahh, a bread snapper, ah God help ya. How old?'

Betty's voice was back to her laboured drawl.

'Six months.'

'Ahhh Jasus! Boy or a child?'

'Girl.'

'I know how ya feel. I have three of me own. But sure don't worry; you'll be out a here in no time arall. I've another year to do an I've been in this hell-hole for nearly three year.' She took toilet paper from beside a pisspot under her bunk and gave it to Mags. 'Come on now, the screws will be around in a few minutes. Whatever ya do, don't let them see ya bawlin'. There's nothing they like better than to see one of us cryin', tellin' ya.'

Mags blew her nose and soon her sobs eased. Fear had made her hungry.

'I'm starvin'. When do we get dinner?'

'Never,' Rosie shouted. 'We get slops in a while. Dey call it stew.'

'Don't mind her, Mags, it's not bad arall.' Betty tried to sound cheerful. 'Better than I get outside, inanyway. Three hot and a cot, sure what more could ya ask for?' She went to Mags and gave her a reassuring hug.

Over Betty's shoulder, Mags saw Rosie's eyes disappear into thick lines of mascara.

'How ja know it's stew today?' Mags asked.

'Stew Monday, Shepherd's Pie Tuesday,' Rosie chanted, 'spuds, peas and chops Wednesday, bacon and cabbage Thursday, fish, beans an' chips Friday, lasagne Saturday, chicken an' roasters Sunday.'

'Jasus, sounds great to me.'

'Ya? Well it all tastes the fuckin' same.'

'Don't mind her, Mags; she's always complainin'.'

'Fuck off you! So would you be complainin' if you were stuck in this kip for the next eight fuckin' year.'

There was a rasping noise and Rice pushed open the door.

'Fall in.'

Mags followed the other two out. The hall was now full of women. Some of the prisoners eyed up Mags in an eerie sort of a way. Others showed no interest. Mags tried her best to look unconcerned, to give the impression of being cool and self-confident, but she was frightened.

The landing, as she would learn to call it, was now a noisy hive of activity. Forty women prisoners slouched about. Towering over them were ten blue-clad officers, mostly women. The smell of hot food competed with the smell of piss and disinfectant.

Everyone seemed to be shouting.

'Got a roll up, Jacinta?'

'Fuck off you. I'm fed up a given ya stuff, ri'?'

'There's no need to get ya bleedin' knickers in a twist.'

'Here! Who robbed me fuckin' hairbrush? '

'I have ya bleedin' hairbrush. Only borried it but, for fuck's sake.'

Officers and prisoners shouted at one another. Cell doors crashed, barred gates smashed.

Disorientated by the ear-splitting confusion of metallic noises, Mags followed her cell mates and the three women stood in line with pisspots in their hands, waiting for the only toilet. As each woman got to the top of the queue, she emptied her pot down an open drain and then used the toilet, the little door hiding her midriff only. When her turn came, Mags had a quick piss, thanking Jesus she had put on clean knickers that morning. She was getting used to using the toilet in front of an audience.

Pulling up her clothes as quickly as possible, she ran after Betty and Rosie but, realising that this would convey the wrong impression, slowed to what she hoped looked like a carefree swagger. She caught up as they left their pots back into the cell and joined another queue.

Mags was given a dinner through the hatch and followed the others back to the cell, where they were locked in. They sat on the edge of the bunks with their trays on their knees. Rosie and Betty started picking at their food. Mags wolfed into her stew, but after a few mouthfuls slowed down. There was a dessert which Mags enjoyed. Having finished her own, Rosie stretched over to Betty's tray and took her dessert. Betty did not seem in the least bit interested. They left their trays beside the door and drank their mugs of tea.

'Any dust?' Rosie asked Mags.

'Dust?'

'Tobacco, for fuck's sake.'

'No.'

'Jasus, ya useless.'

'Here, I have.' Betty held up a packet of tobacco.

'Any skins?'

'No, use the buke.'

A torn Bible, the only book in the cell, lay on the floor in a corner. Betty ripped out a page. As Rosie rolled a cigarette and crumbled hash into it, Betty read from the Bible in a singsong voice.

'When I consider thy Heavens, the work of thy fingers, the muan and the stars, which thou hast ordained; what is man, that thou art mindful of him? and the son of man, that thou visitest him? For thou hast made him little lower than the angels, and hast crowned him with glory and honour. Thou madest him to have dominion over the works of thy hands; thou hast ...'

'Shut ta fuck up, an' get some a that inta ya before the screws is around again for fall in.'

Betty took the joint, sucked in greedily and held the smoke in her lungs as she spoke to Mags.

'We get two hours now for exercise, or laundry or school.'

'School?' Mags asked.

'Ya, school, so what?' Rosie challenged.

'I wanna go to school.' Mags sounded adamant.

'For wha'?'

'To improve meself.'

Rosie glared. 'Wha'? We not good enough for ya?'

'Leave her alone. She's right ta go ta school.' Betty finally exhaled. 'It's better than hangin' round the laundry all day talkin' about all the great strokes we've done, or walkin round in circles talkin' shit.'

'That so now? Well talkin' shit was good enough for you til little Miss Snotty Nose arrived.'

'Leave it out, Rosie. Don't mind her, Mags. You go ta school, there's nothing better ta do. Can ya read an write?'

Mags shook her head.

'There ya are then. They'll learn ya in no time in the school here, honest. Myself an most of the girls learned in here, tellin' ya.'

'Yea?' Rosie's tone was ugly. 'Well I never read a buke in me life an I'm worth ten times more money than any of them scumbag teachers.'

'Still, Rosie, sure there's nothin' wrong with a bit a learnin'.'

'Lot a good it will do you.'

Rosie stressed the 'you' strangely and Betty's head dropped. There was a malignant silence.

Mags started to pace the cell. She could take four steps before turning.

'Leave it out! Stop, ta fuck will ya?' Rosie pointed a finger at Mags. 'Don't tell me that ya goin' to be one a them silly fuckers that can't do bird.' She looked over to Betty. 'If she's goin' to be one a them, I'll get her ta fuck out a here fast. She can go in with the bleedin' knackers. They all go off their fuckin' heads when they're inside inanyway, so another won't make any differ.' Rosie chuckled. 'Gets like a fuckin' slaughterhouse whenever the knackers start slashing themselves.'

Mags was getting pissed off with Rosie, but she sat down. Looking round the cell, she saw a small portable radio and turned it on. It was crackly and at full volume it could barely be heard.

'We need new batteries, love.' Betty sounded depressed. The news crackled from the radio.

'Turn that shit off,' Rosie demanded.

Mags went to switch it off as the newsreader started a report. 'In the Central Criminal Court today, Paul Robinson of Patrick Pearse flats was sentenced to five years' penal servitude for armed robbery.'

'Sshh. Leave it on.'

'Garda witness Sergeant Michael Murphy had earlier told the court that Robinson had been arrested outside the Ulster Bank in Baggot Street in possession of the stolen money and that he had been armed with an iron bar. Defending solicitor James Hargroves told the judge that Robinson had a drug problem, that he had since begun a programme in Coolmine Rehabilitation Centre and that the defendant was now leading a useful and drug-free life with his wife and children. His client greatly regretted the crime which he had committed to pay for his drug habit. In sentencing Robinson, Judge O'Brien said that the best drug rehabilitation programme that he could think of for the defendant was a five-year stay in Mountjoy Prison, where Robinson would have ample opportunity to meditate on the trouble he had landed himself into with his use of drugs.'

'Jasus! Robbo's back in again. Poor Helen.'

'In the Dáil today the Ceann Comhairle refused time to discuss the collapse of the Insurance Corporation of Ireland. Earlier in the House, the Minister for Finance would not be drawn on the question of the £90 million which it is reported that the government intend to grant to the company to offset their losses. In reply –'

'Will ya turn off that shit an' save the batteries?'

Mags turned off the radio and started to pace again.

Rosie lugged her large body off the bunk and stood in front of her.

'Sit down.'

They were standing so close together that Mags could smell Rosie's rancid breath.

Mags was so frightened she could feel her heart race, but she stared back.

'Fuck off you an' leave me alone. Ri'?'

Rosie's face paled under the make-up. Mags braced herself for action, but the tension was dissipated by the door being thrown open by a very young-looking officer. Her spotless uniform hung from her and her cap appeared to be several sizes too big.

'Fall in.'

Craning her neck out from the bottom bunk, Betty shouted, 'Jasus, look at it! How old are you? Twelve? You'll be gettin' tits next.'

As they filed out of the cell, Officer Rice came over to the new officer whose face was glowing red. She nodded in the direction of the departing prisoners.

'Don't let them get to you, Officer Kavanagh. They're not half as tough as they would like you to think they are. Just don't let them see any weakness, or you're a gonner. Be fair, be tough, stick to the letter of the rules and you'll be OK.'

Every other prisoner had scurried towards a male officer who wore a white cotton coat over his uniform, so Mags got the use of the toilet without queuing. As soon as she sat on the metal toilet, however, another prisoner was standing outside the door.

'Hurry ta fuck outa there, I'm burstin'!'

She didn't need to be told twice. In a flash, her clothes were rearranged and she was out of the toilet.

Of the prisoners milling around the white-coated officer, Rosie was getting near him quickest, Betty in her slipstream. Chaos reigned. Agitated prisoners argued with the officer, who was handing out pills and liquid in little plastic tubs. Mags noticed several women take tablets, pretend to put them into their mouths and surreptitiously drop them into their pockets. She was amazed to see Rosie and Betty given a fistful of pills each. She noticed Rosie hide hers, as Betty downed pills like a spoilt child with Smarties.

'What's all that stuff, Betty?'

'Medication. Come on.'

29

She led Mags into a small room off the landing in which a telly was blaring out pop videos. The television was encased in a metal box with scratched and burned perspex in front of the screen. A handsome, bronzed man in a frilly shirt sang to a beautiful young woman who was on the balcony of a castle. The lyrics were sad: he had to leave her. As he got into a silver BMW, tears rolled down the woman's face.

'How come their mascara never runs on telly?' Betty sounded indignant. 'Here, fuck this, I'm goin' to the yard. Ya comin'?'

The song was Mags' favourite, but she felt safe with Betty and followed her out.

The exercise yard was a small tarmacadamed square. Two sides were fenced by mesh, topped with razor wire. Footballs were impaled on the wire. Beyond this mesh were huge grey walls. The other sides of the yard were bordered by two wings of the prison.

Mags noticed that most of the windows had some mesh missing and many of the panes of glass were broken. The ground under the windows was littered with bundled-up newspapers, many of which had burst open, displaying a core of shit. The smell wafted over the yard.

Surely ta Jasus women don't shit out here, Mags thought, but was too embarrassed to ask Betty.

Heads could be seen at the windows of the fellas' cells. A dozen shouted conversations were going on, all at once, with the women in the yard, as they slouched around in circles. Between the mesh, the bars and the dirt on the glass, the faces could not be seen. She wondered how the women knew which voice was directed to them, but they seemed to have no problem untangling the web of conversations.

A skinny young one, about Mags' age, was dragging her feet around with an enormous effort. She was behind Mags, who couldn't help staring around at her. She looked as white as – no, not white, she was a pale green colour, only her lips were white. Across her throat were three thick, purple scars.

She caught Mags staring at her, but her glazed eyes registered no interest. Her eyelids drooped heavily and it appeared she was about to collapse.

Mags was jolted out of her thoughts by a young one who bellowed above the other conversations, 'Snake?'

'Wha'?'

'Get up on ya springs, Snake.'

'What's the story?'

'Nuttin', sept I love ya, Snake.'

'I love ya too, Nanno.'

'Ya better.'

'You threatenin' me? Ya titless cunt ya.'

'No.'

'Ya fuckin' well better not. Ri'?'

'Why not? Ya poxy scumbag ya.'

'Snort dat, fuck face.'

'I'm afraid a you, ya shitty poxhead ya.'

'Yea? Well just watch it, ri'?'

'What ya mean titless anyhow?'

'Was only jokin', they're coming along great. De must be feedin' ya Bloom down there.'

'I love ya, Snake.'

'I love ya, Nanno.'

Definitely getting their lines crossed, Mags thought. The bellowing young one had a chest as smooth as a Dublin Bay flatfish.

A woman with a determined set to her jaw ran around the little yard as if trying to put distance between herself and the prison.

'What's the story with your woman that's running, Betty? Does she think she might get up enough speed to fly outa here?'

'She'll be flyin' nowhere for years an' years. Tells everyone she's in for drugs. She killed an awl one for the fiver in her bag. See ya woman there?' Betty pointed out a woman whom Mags thought looked about seventy years old. 'Her fella used ta kick the shit outa her, an' one night she stabbed him fifty times with the bread knife. They say it was supposed ta be once for every beatin' he gave her, but that she ran outa energy. Died roarin', so he did.'

'What's the story with yourself an' Rosie?'

'I got five year for possession a heroin with intent ta supply. I'd only enough for myself an' a few a me friends but. Rosie copped ten year. She was caught with nearly a million pound worth.'

'A million bleedin' pound worth? Jasus! I'd never take any a that stuff, Betty. You'd wanna be mad. Kills ya.'

'Yea, kills ya.' Betty went quiet.

As verbal warfare raged between windows and yard, Mags wondered where Tracy was now. Did she miss her mammy as much as she missed her little angel? Christ! She'd give anything for a hug from Tracy.

Deep in her sombre thoughts, she ceased to notice the profanities flying through the air, the declarations of hate intermixed with professions of love and lust – courteous words of seduction, blended with nauseating expressions of debauchery.

The babble of exchanges congealed into a chorus of cheers and catcalls and the new rhythm jolted Mags' mind back to the prison yard. She nearly bumped into the scar-throated prisoner. She was standing facing the windows with her tracksuit bottoms and knickers down around her ankles. A male voice shouted above the noise of the hilarity from the windows.

'Come on, tits an' all, or no deal. Ri'?'

She lifted her tracksuit top and exposed two drooping breats; they reminded Mags of pictures of famine in Africa. Below the barren breasts were two long irregular-shaped wounds and abscesses covered her lower abdomen and legs. Blood rushed to Mags' head. Without thinking, she pulled the clothes back into place. The blank-eyed woman did not resist as Mags rearranged her garments.

Over a chorus of obscenities, a voice from the windows shouted. 'Fair play ta ya, Amanda. A deal's a deal; here's the bit a shit I promised ya.'

A balled-up sheet of newspaper was thrown from the window and exploded on landing. Shit flew in all directions, splashing several of the women. Shrieks of laughter came from the windows.

Mags was roughly pushed away by Officer Rice, who grabbed the reluctant flasher and frog-marched her back to the prison building.

'In the name of God, have you no shame at all? You're for the pad if you do anything disgusting like that again. Do you hear me now?'

Amanda gave no indication of having heard, as, stumbling, she was dragged away.

'Ay Betty,' a voice Mags had not heard before, shouted from a window. 'Who's the new bit a stuff in the Rasherhouse?'

'Mind ya own fuckin' business, Dommo.'

'Ay young one, what's ya name?'

'Mind your own business.' Mags knew her voice did not convey the hardened tone she would have liked.

'Ah come on. I've been watching ya an' I really fancy ya. What do they call ya?'

'Mags.'

'Can I ask for a visit to ya, Mags?'

'Don't care if ya do or not.'

'Great! Thanks! Hafta go. See ya, Mags.'

'Watch yourself with ya man,' Betty warned. 'He's a fine bit a stuff, but he's a bad bastard.'

'What's he in for?'

'Killed a guy in a knife fight. He's due out soon.'

'How old's he?'

''Bout twenty-two.'

The reader can see from the above text, I am sure, the wisdom of Bentham's insistence that there should be no communication between prisoners. The full tragedy of not implementing this policy will slowly unfold as the story progresses. Under the misguided demand for a more 'humane' treatment for prisoners, their real interests have been sacrificed on the altar of the so-called rehabilitation model for prisons. This is the model so beloved of the radical feminists. Being 'progressive', they cannot resist the desire to appear enlightened on matters about which they know absolutely nothing.

But before the true tragedy caused by these misguided ideas transpires, let me give the reader a brief history of the prison reform debate.

Among a plethora of ideas about crime and punishment, two schools of thought are most prominent: the Classical School of Criminology and the Positivist School. About the latter I shall speak anon.

The first criminologists have come to be called the classical criminologists. They based their ideas on the Social Contract. Crudely stated, the Social Contract holds that before the advent of organised society, people's lives were, in the words of that great philosopher Thomas Hobbes, 'solitary, poor, nasty, brutish, and short'. To escape this state of affairs, people voluntarily gave up some rights in return for protection and the guarantee of others.

It was necessary to defend the Social Contract from those who would encroach on the rights of others. Punishments that strike the senses were necessary to prevent the despotism of each individual from plunging society into its former chaos; they were established to discourage transgressions of the law. Laws and punishments were necessary to counterbalance the effects of the passions of the individual which opposed the general good. Neither the power of eloquence nor the sublimest truths are sufficient to restrain these passions. Without laws, society would dissolve back to brutish chaos.

The Classical Theory could be summed up by saying: All men, being by nature self-seeking, are liable to commit crime. There is a consensus in society as to the desirability of protecting private property and personal welfare. In order to prevent a war of all against all, men freely enter into a contract with the state to preserve the peace.

Punishments must be used to deter the individual from violating the interests of others, and not for reformation, which would encroach on the rights of the individual and transgress the social contract. The individual is responsible for his actions and is equal, no matter what his rank, in the eyes of the law. Mitigating circumstances or excuses are therefore inadmissible.

As the nineteenth century progressed, the Classical School became associated with the rising middle class and Liberalism. Liberalism has the redeeming feature that it does not subscribe to any silly utopian philosophy of absolute equality. The classical criminologists believed, rightly, in equality between those who contribute equally to society. As Hobbes said, the poor would see the justice of the social contract. And prisons, I would add, are there for those who choose depravity.

These are the ideas which frame the thinking behind Irish prison policy today, or should I say 'did', until the authorities had to bow to pressure groups. These groups' ideas are guided, if they are guided at all, by Positivism. Later, at an appropriate point in the text, I shall discuss the Positivist ideas, but for now back to the characters who best illustrate, albeit unintentionally, the foolishness of departing from the wisdom of the classical ideas on prison.

Fall in was called and they all filed back onto the landing. Tea was given out at the hatch and Mags followed Betty and Rosie back to the cell where they were locked in for the night. Having eaten the choicest bits off her own plate, Rosie grazed Betty's abandoned meal, then turned a predatory eye on Mags' food. Mags forced herself to finish the contents of the plate.

'Don't know how ya can eat that slop,' Rosie shouted.

'Ya made a good try yourself, all the same,' Mags replied. 'It's not that bad.'

'Ya mustanta seen the kitchen.'

The half-empty plates were left near the door and the three women lay down on their bunks. Mags had a choice of either of the top ones. Choosing the one over Betty's, she wondered if they would be able to breathe at all if someone was put into the cell for the fourth bed. Lying on her back, she stared at the domed ceiling, then turned on her stomach, then on to her back again.

'How ja get out to the toila?'

'Ya don't till eight tomorra mornin'.'

'Wha'?'

'Tomorra.'

'Jasus, what'll I do?'

'There's a pisspot under the bunk there.'

Mags got off her bunk and started to pace her cell. 'But I'm dying for ... ya know ...'

'Ah for Jasus' sake,' Rosie roared at her, 'don't tell me ya didn't do it before comin' in? An stop that walkin' up an down, will ya?'

'Can't.'

'Well ya better or I'll burst ya.'

'Leave her alone, Rosie. Sure she's not used ta being in jail an' she's upset about the snapper and all.'

Betty sat up on the bunk and taking Mags' hand gently, guided her to sit beside her. Rosie sat up and craned her neck until her fat face was only inches from Betty's.

'Don't you go gettin' all lovey dovey with little snotty nose now, ri'?'

'Rosie, she's only a kid!'

'Look I'm burstin', what'll I do?'

'Ya afraid we'll find out ya shit smells the same as everyone else's?'

'Leave her alone, Rosie. Here, Mags, you're lucky, I have a newspaper here. Ya can use dat.'

'Wha'?'

36

'Ya have ta do it on dat. Then ya can fuck it out the winda like. Otherwise we'll suffocate.'

Betty moved one of the lockers to form a screen, placed the newspaper on the floor and turned the radio on as loud as the failing batteries would allow. She put a pisspot into the space she had made.

'Now, love, you'll be fine. Use the pot for a piss first but.'

Mags squatted over the newspaper. The face of an obese cleric smiled piously up at her. Despite her urgency and distress, somehow it didn't seem right. Quickly she turned the page to where huge black print announced: 'Randy Vicar in Wild Sex Romp'. She relieved herself on the picture underneath of a girl about her own age wearing only black lace knickers and a priest's collar. The girl's face was mouthing 'Ohhh'.

'Has anyone a loan of a pad?' The shame and indignity brought Mags near to tears. Betty threw her one.

'There ya are, ya poor little love ya. Now bundle it all up an' fuck it out the winda.'

Metal shrieked on concrete as Betty heaved a bunk beneath the window.

'An 'urry up for 'uck's sake,' Rosie shouted, holding her nose.

As Mags managed to force the parcel out of the hole in the mesh, Betty shouted, 'There ya are, Rice, a little present for ya.'

'Ya scumbag ya,' Rosie added.

Mags climbed down from the bunk and Bettty climbed up. She went to shout out the bars, then stopped.

'Here, gis up a bit a bogroll.'

She wiped the bars and threw the toilet paper out shouting, 'Dommo, what's the story?'

After a pause a voice came from above.

'No bleedin' story.'

'Don't give me dat! I know ya had a visit.'

'I told ya, no fuckin' story. Ri'?'

'Ya bleedin' useless so ya are.'

'Ya not bleedin' brilliant with stories yourself dees days, are ya?'

Betty whispered down to Rosie. 'Stupa bollix has nothin'' then yelled back through the window again. 'I'm dyin' for a bit a news from the outside. I'm sick with the worry, ja hear me, sick with the worry.'

'Honest, haven't heard antin from me family for ages.'

Betty got down from the window.

'Scumbag, bet ya he has shitloads. Down to emergency rations, I suppose. Wha' ya got left, Rosie?'

'I got the six Naps. You want any, Mags?'

Mags had no idea what a Nap was, but she felt sure it was best to refuse.

'I've no money.'

'Don't be stupa, that's all arranged outside.'

'No. Thanks all the same.'

'Ya sure, love?' Rosie was sickly sweet.

'Sure.'

'C'mere ta me, love.' Rosie's voice was still treacly. 'If ya tell the screws that ya in the horrors, they'll give ya Phy for the next six weeks, an' if ya don't want it, I'll pay ya well for it.'

'What are ya talkin' about?'

'Look, if you tell them that you're in the horrors cos a withdrawin' from heroin, they'll give ya Phyceptone, so they will, an' if ya don't want it, I'll take it an' have two hundred pound sent to whoever ya want.'

'Sure they know I'm not on heroin.'

'No look, we'd give ya a few marks on your arms, tracks like, an' those idiots wouldn't know the differ.'

'Tracks?'

'A few pricks with me sewin' needle and then rub them to make dem look sore. Wouldn't hurt a bit, honest.'

'It's no good, Rosie,' Betty piped in. 'Sure they would watch her takin' it. She wouldn't be able ta give them ya anyway.'

'She would. She could keep them under her tongue,

pretend ta swallow, an give them ta me after.'

'They would give it to her in a liquid.'

'Anyway I won't, so forget it,' Mags said firmly.

Rosie turned sour.

'Dat so, Little Miss Stuck Up? That's OK, don't bother your bollix then. It's your baby you're worried 'bout, not mine.'

'Come on, Rosie.' Betty was becomming anxious. 'Get's a Nap for fuck's sake before I lose me reason altogether. If I don't get some real gear soon, I'll do myself in, I swear.'

'Sshh! Some scumbag's at the spyhole again.' Rosie moved towards the door.

'Jasus, it's disgustin'-lookin'!' Mags was looking at the hole in the door. She never realised how ugly an eye could look. Seeing no eyebrow, eyelash or face, all she was aware of was a moist dark area surrounded by bloodshot yellowy white. The unblinking eye looked like a discoloured oyster, a malevolent living part of the grey door. She shivered.

'Bet ya it's dat scumbag Paddy, tryin' to get his rocks off, hoping ta see sometin spicy.' Rosie put her eye up to the hole and stared back, shouting, 'Ya poxy awl scumbag ya.' Then in a lower voice. 'Won't be back for a while. Ya ri'?'

Rosie took a large pink hairbrush, dragged it through her crispy blonde hair a few times, then beat a tattoo on the heating pipes which ran along the end wall of the cell at floor level. Similar rhythms were transmitted from cell to cell.

'Ri',' she said, putting down the brush, 'coast is clear.'

As Betty stood with her back to the door, covering the spyhole, Rosie took down her tracksuit bottoms and her knickers. She squatted down and, with an air of professional disinterest, inserted two fingers deep into her vagina. Mags turned to the wall in disgust as Rosie, still fishing in her own body, talked business to Betty.

'Your bleedin' account's gettin' fuckin' high, remember?'

'Look, aren't I out in another year?'

Rosie pulled a condom from her body, took a large

39

chalky tablet out of it and threw it to Betty. She reinserted the bulging condom and pulled up her clothes.

Betty crushed the tablet and arranged the white dust in a line on the bedside table. Rosie held up a cheap biro.

'Do go to school myself sometimes, so I do.' She slipped the cylinder from around the ink tube and handed it to Betty. 'Where do ya think I get me pens?'

'Not that ya bleedin' learned anything,' Betty said, and snorted half of the white line up her nose through the cylinder, then transferring it to her other nostril, inhaled the last of the chalky substance.

Rosie was starting to undress.

'Wha' ya mean, not that I learned anything? *Dún do bhéal agus ná bí* a cunt all your life.'

In mock aggression she grabbed Betty, who laughed loudly and hugged her.

'Leave it out, Rosie, an' let's get ta bed before the scumbags put the lights out.'

Mags undressed quickly, putting the prison nightdress on over the teeshirt, bra and pants. She climbed onto the top bunk. Lying there, she couldn't help but notice the other two strip naked. Both women resembled creatures who had emerged from under a boulder, never having seen the sun. They were sickly white. Rosie's whiteness was accentuated by spaghetti junctions of bright blue veins. Big and solid, she dwarfed Betty, who was emaciated and whose empty breasts hung over prominent ribs; tattooed messages on her arms were punctuated by sores and boils.

Mags turned to the wall to escape the sight to which her eyes had been drawn, but which made her stomach churn. She tried to imaginge her baby, warm and safe in her mother's flat, but the image wouldn't come. She kept seeing disturbing scenes in which Tracy was in distress and crying out for her.

The lights went out without warning, leaving only a small grid of moonlight stretched across one wall.

'God oh God keep my little baby safe,' she prayed, but

as she drifted towards sleep, she heard the sound of her child crying. She slept fitfully, then jolted fully awake. Disorientated, she was aware of a terrible nightmare. Focusing on the dim grid of light on the wall, she realised that the nightmare was her stark reality. The cell was devoid of air, and an oppressive claustrophobia brought out beads of sweat all over her body.

Prisoners were shouting from their windows, but in time, she began to doze off with the shouted abuse battering her brain.

Mags bolted upright in her bunk. Above the shouting, she could definitely hear crying. Had someone brought the baby into the cell? Was she going mad? Peering in the direction of the whimpering sounds, her eyes became accustomed to the dark.

Dim squares of light illuminated the bunk opposite. Blankets were strewn around the floor and the grey squares showed a mound of flesh like a headless octopus squirming on the bed. With a sickening sensation in her stomach, Mags realised that the whimpering was not from her or from anyone else's baby. The women's heads were buried between each other's thighs. A sheen of sweat shone in the grey light as Rosie and Betty squirmed rhythmically.

From a nearby cell a high-pitched scream slashed the darkness. Mags spun back to the wall. She squeezed the pillow over her head and cried silently.

'For fuck's sake, get back to bed,' Rosie glared venomously at Mags. 'I haven't had a wink a sleep in the week you've been here, with your traipsing up an' down like a fuckin' yo yo. I'll bleedin' do for ya if ya don't leave it out. Ja hear me? Do ya?'

Rosie turned towards the wall abruptly, almost knocking Betty out of the bunk.

The door rasped open.

'Slop out,' Officer Kavanagh said, trying to make her youthful voice authoritative.

Grabbing her pisspot, Mags rushed out, emptied it, and took her place in the queue for the shower. In the vain hope of taking a shower without an audience, she had struggled against her instinct for cleanliness until her cell's putrid smell seemed to have penetrated her skin. She could not put it off any longer.

When her turn came, she stripped quickly, hoping that the steamy hot water would hide her embarrassment. She faced in during the shower and, stepping out backwards, put on her nightdress without drying.

On her way back to the cell, Mags passed Rosie and Betty in the queue.

'Jasus,' she murmured to Betty, 'you'd think they would put up a curtain on the bleedin' shower.'

'No way. Sure ya might enjoy it then. Anyway, sure that's the only way Paddy can get hisself a hard-on.'

As she went into the cell, Mags shouted across the landing to Officer Kavanagh. 'Will ya make sure I'm called for school today, please?'

'I will of course, Margaret.'

In the queue Rosie turned to Betty, smiling broadly. 'Will ya make sure I'm called for school, officer dear?' she mimicked sweetly. Smile and sweetness vanished. 'That little cunt will be grassin' next, tellin' ya.'

There was the usual jostling to get medication from the white-suited officer. Then the prisoners were locked in the cells with their breakfasts.

Betty barely touched her food. She lay on the bunk, her hands behind her head. Mags could not eat either. The others had not rinsed out their pisspots. That and the plastic bag full of dirty underwear in the corner did not help her appetite.

She took her tray off her knees and put the uneaten breakfast by the door.

'Ay come here, Betty.' Mags was staring at Betty's arms. 'Ja have a car crash, or what?'

'Car crash?'

'Your arms, all a them scars on your arms.'

Betty looked at the scars. Some were small and short, but there were six on her left arm which were as thick as pencils and practically went the full round of her arm. Her right arm had only two long gashes, but like the left, there was little unscarred tissue to be seen.

'No, I didn't have a bleedin' car crash.'

'What happened ya then?'

'Leave it out, will ya Mags?'

Betty was annoyed, but after a short silence, she mellowed.

'Me head gets fucked up betimes.'

'Wha' ja mean?'

'I done them meself.'

'Ya wha'?'

'I done them meself, I told ya!' Betty was getting annoyed again. 'Ya deaf or wha? Sure wha' else would I do in this kip, day in day out, year in year out, but try ta do meself in?'

'Jasus!'

'Yea well.'

'Ya mean ya tried ta kill yourself dozens a times?'

'Yea. Now get out a me face. Ri'.' Betty screeched at Mags, than she rolled, face down on the bunk and broke into a fit of sobbing.

Mags felt sorry for having brought up the subject. She sat over on Betty's bunk and put her hand on her shoulder.

'Hey, Mother fuckin' Teresa, get ya hands off!' Rosie wrenched Mags's hand from Betty and kept a grip of her wrist as she stared threateningly at her. Mags looked back defiantly, then, jerking her hand free, kept her fist on a level with Rosie's head. They eyed each other. Mags was breathing rapidly. She was sure that Rosie was about to hit out, but she didn't care. If she didn't stand up for herself now, she knew that the rest of her time inside would be made a misery. Win or lose, she was determined to fight.

'Just watch it, ri'?' Rosie's words sounded tough, but

were tantamount to a backdown. She began to roll a cigarette.

Betty had stopped sobbing and was looking wide-eyed at the confrontation. When the tension eased, she spoke.

'Didn't really want ta kill meself. Well that's wha' the psycho says anyhow. Could have fooled me but, so he could. I would have loved to end it all, dozens a times. Suppose I hadn't the bottle.'

Mags was incredulous. 'How ja do it?'

'Blades, broken mirrors, broken mugs – antin' I could get me hands on.'

Mags held her own wrists.

'Jasus Christ! You're bleedin' mad, so ya are. I'd never do a thing like that.'

Betty was beginning to warm to her subject, enjoying the attention.

'That's why we all have plastic cups an' plates now, an' plastic knives and forks.'

She pulled her teeshirt up, exposing five purple scars running across her stomach.

'Dem three were the babbies; that one was the spoon an' that one was the three batteries.'

'Spoons an' batteries? What ya talkin' about, for Jasus' sake?'

'I had ta be operated on to have them taken out a me stomach.'

'How in the name a Jasus did they get in there in the first place?'

'I ate them, of course! I ate the spoon at a different time than the batteries but. I swallied three big batteries all at the one time, so I did.'

'Why in the name a fuck ja do that?'

'Well the spoon was a bet, ya know like. But they have ta bring ya to the hospital ta get it out, so ya have a break from this kip. You'd do antin' after a while ta get out a here. They're lovely over in the hospital. Treat ya like a queen, an' the food's only gorgeous. The time I ate the batteries, I got

44

the Christmas out of it. Me an' the screw, Rice, guardin' me. We had a great time. On Christmas day me Ma brought the kids up an some of the girls came as well. We all got pissed, including the screw. She was really nice then, not like now, poxy scumbag. Jasus, she nearly got sacked but. There was murder in the hospital ward that night between us all an' the matron. Jasus, it was great crack. Best Christmas I ever had.'

Betty was becoming animated. A delicate flush of colour showed on her sickly white face. Having an audience gave her a buzz. 'See this one here?' she giggled, pointing to one of the bigger scars on her left arm. 'That's ...' She stopped dead. The look of her mutilated arms brought her back to reality with a bang and she spoke out loud to herself. 'Leave it out, ya fuckin eejit ya, Betty.'

Mags tried to think of something to say to cheer up Betty again.

'Anyone for a roll-up?'

'Me, Mags,' Betty muttered.

'Here's the skins.' Rosie threw a packet of cigarette papers onto Mags' lap.

Including Rosie in the offer of a roll-up was Mags' peace offering, and Rosie's acceptance signalled a lull in hostilities.

Mags rolled her own cigarette with ease, if not the speedy expertise of the others. Passing on her tobacco pouch and skins, she took a drag. She was nearly finished her second ounce of tobacco since coming in. So much for her year off the fags, she thought. Anyway, she would give them up again when she got out.

Mags watched the smoke lazily curl and coil in the dull square of light afforded by the window. She could barely see Betty's face, but she sensed that she was still depressed.

'What do all the tattoos say, Betty?'

'Mother, rest in peace.' Betty pointed to an agonised head of Jesus with a crown of thorns. Fat drops of crimson blood dripped down her shoulder.

'I got that the day me poor Mammy died, God rest her soul.'

'Have ya got one for ya Da, or is he still alive?'

Betty put her head out over the edge of the bed and spat on the floor.

Confused, Mags pointed to a tattoo on Betty's collar bone. An arrow pierced a haemorrhaging red heart. Blood flowed onto the words. 'Anto and Betty for ever'.

'Who's Anto?'

'A fella a mine. Bleedin' gorgeous. Spittin' image of Elvis; everyone said so. Had him eatin' out of me hand, do antin' for me he would. Loved me so much, he'd be driven into a frenzy if I so much as looked at another fella. He'd an awful temper.'

'Ya still with him?'

'Fucked off with a sixteen-year-old, dirty awl bollix.' Betty put her fist up to Mags' face. The letters HATE were tattooed below the knuckles, one letter to each finger. 'I'd give him dat I would. Look but.' She held up her other fist and showed the letters LOVE. 'Ja like dem?'

'Great.' Mags tried to sound convincing.

'I can do them. I'll give ya any ya want.'

'Wha'?'

'Tattoos.'

'You can do tattoos?'

'Yea. Ja want one?'

'Not now thanks.'

'Ya have ta have ya borstal mark but.'

'Me wha'?'

'Borstal mark, for Jasus' sake,' Rosie shouted. 'Ya deaf or wha'? Everyone that comes in here gets one.' Rosie pointed to a small black mark on her cheekbone.

'That way we all know one another. One big happy family, like, ya wide?'

'See mine.' Betty pointed to a misshapen blotch on her face.

'Ja like it?'

'Lovely. How ja do them?'

'Seasy. Ya draw the picture ya want on your skin, ri'?

46

Then ya wind some thread round the point of a needle, dip it in ink every now an' then, an just jab it up an' down along the drawin'. Ya get all these little scabs, an after a few days they fall off an there's ya tattoo.'

'Sounds awful so it does.'

'Only hurts a bit, like, an' it's worth it. Isn't it worth it, Rosie? Show her the one I did on you.'

Rosie pulled up her teeshirt and yanked down her bra, exposing a big blue rose on her breast. Taking a deep breath, she stuck her chest into Mags' face, causing her to back away to focus on what she first took to be an ugly birthmark.

'Ja like it?' Rosie shook her body and grinned broadly.

''S'lovely. Pity there's pricks on it but.'

Rosie's grin disappeared. Glaring at Mags, she rearranged her bra.

'Will I give ya a borstal mark, Mags? T'would look great on ya, honest. Wouldn't it, Rosie?'

'Ya can put it on her arse for all I care. Stuck up little cunt thinks she's too good for a borstal spot. Wouldn't look right in the fancy job she's going to get when she leaves this kip.' Rosie started to mimic in a posh accent. 'Will you please make sure I'm called for school, officer dear.' Then with venom. 'Tellin' ya, she'll be grassin' next.'

'Ah don't say that, sure isn't she right ta want ta better herself.'

'Listen you.' Mags stood up and looked Rosie in the eye. 'I'm no grass, ri'? Maybe your kids never got any schoolin', but my baby –'

'My kids go to the best schools in Dublin, I'll have ya know,' Rosie interrupted, shoving her face up to Mags'.

'Yea? Well I don't know how ya manage that, but I intend ta work for the good a me baby an' that means I'll need a bit a schoolin', ri'?'

Rosie moved her face even closer to Mags'. 'What do you mean insultin' me an mine?' she hissed. 'I'm a hard-working businesswoman an' I won't have a snotty-nosed little cunt like you making accusations.'

The door opened and Kavanagh shouted for fall in. Rosie barged out knocking Mags onto the bunk. Mags got up and kicked the end wall so hard, she thought she had broken her big toe. Grabbing her foot, she hopped back to the bunk, and began to cry.

'Now now, Margaret, it can't be as bad as all that.' Mags could just see Kavanagh's face, through her tears. 'This might cheer you up.' She gave Mags an envelope.

'What's that?'

'A letter, can't you see?'

'From who?'

'I don't know.' The envelope had been torn open. 'It's from someone in the prison.'

'Read it for us will ya? I haven't got me glasses in here with me an' I'm as blind as a bleedin' bat without dem.'

'Right.' Officer Kavanagh took out the letter and looked at the last page. 'It's from someone called Dommo. A friend of yours?'

'Yea a friend. I've been talkin' to him at the windows an' we had a half hour in the visitin' box yesterday. Jasus, I couldn't believe it when I saw him. He's gorgeous, an' really nice, so he is. Sure you were in the box, ya saw him yourself.'

'Oh him? Yes, I've heard about your friend Dommo all right.' She started to read.

'"My darling Mags." Huh! Some friend! "You have changed my whole life. Seeing you in the yard and talking to you out the window, I just knew you were something special. Then the minute I met you yesterday I fell madly in love with you. Mags darling, I adore you with all my heart."'

'Jasus!' Instinctively, Mags put her hands over her cheeks to hide her embarrassment.

'Jasus, is right. "I have been in this poxy cell for two and a half years now for a crime I ..." The next bit is censored.'

'Censored. Wha's that?'

'It means that all letters are checked for things that might endanger security, and anything they feel isn't suitable is blacked out so that it can't be read. There are only a few bits censored here.'

'Ya mean dat all our letters are read by the screws?'

'By the officers! Yes.'

'Toe-rags!'

'Listen, Margaret, if you're going to be abusive, I won't read any more. Do you want me to continue?'

'Yes please.'

'No more name-calling, then. "Mags, I just couldn't believe my luck. After the visit I was in a dream. I just lay on my bunk looking up at the poster of Samantha Fox and thinking what an ugly bag she was in comparison to you, my darling. For the first time ever, I have something to look forward to. I don't care if you do have a kid. I'll still love you and it. Don't worry about losing your Corporation house, Mags. When I get out, I will get a flat for the three of us and we'll live in bliss. If you get out first, I have money that you can have to get the flat and keep yourself and the kid till I get let out. About that scumbag that made ya pregnant, when I'm released I'll ..." censored, "... kneecaps...', censored, "... balls, one by one." censored.'

Officer Kavanagh flicked through the pages. 'Margaret, there are another four pages of this and with the censoring and all, it's a bit hard to read. You'll have to find someone else to finish it. I'll get into trouble if I'm seen reading for much longer.' She handed the letter to Mags, who took it with the reverence appropriate to a precious manuscript.

'Will ya write him a letter for me, please?'

'I can't. I have to get back onto the landing.'

'Ah pleeease?' Mags was near to tears.

Kavanagh hesitated. The sight of Mags' tearful eyes melted her heart. She smiled and looked pretty, not the po-faced officer Mags had got to know in the last week.

'OK, it will have to be short. Very short indeed.'

'Thanks. You're a pet.' Much to the officer's embarrassment, Mags gave her a big hug.

Kavanagh left the cell and arrived back with an envelope and notebook. She found the centre spread and wrote Mags' name and cell number on it.

'Right, just a note now.'

'My darling love Dommo.'

'Margaret, it's none of my business, I know, but this young man is in here for a series of very violent crimes. You know him from only one visit. His last victim died and he was lucky to get off with manslaughter. Really I think ...'

'He was only a boy when all that happened. He's different now, honest. He swore to me he was.'

Kavanagh raised her eyes to heaven.

'Right! "My darling love Dommo." What's next?'

'"I love you too, love, and I can't wait to get out and we can be happy together."' Mags wrinkled up her face. 'Let's think now. Oh yea! "You will love the kid, she is really beautiful and is no bother, honest. When I get out, I'm going to do a FÁS course in cookery and get a good job. There's great money in cookery these days. Me Ma will help with the kid and when I get a job, it will help pay for the flat."'

'Come on Margaret, we must finish.'

'Ri'. "I love you Dommo with all my heart. I'll stop now because I have to go to school, but I'm only living for our next visit. Mags".'

The young officer folded the page and put it in the envelope.

'Actually I got engaged myself last week, Margaret.'

'Ahh Jasus, ya gettin' married?'

'Not for a few years yet. Paul still has another exam to do before he becomes an accountant, but we've put a deposit on a gorgeous little house in Lucan. He's already moved in and he's doing some repairs in his spare time. It's very small now, but it's really old-fashioned and nice.'

'What's he look like?'

'Well, eh ... he's a bit like the house, I suppose. Small but very nice to look at. He has gorgeous black hair. They don't approve in work, but he has it in a little pigtail.'

'So that's where you've been hiding. Are you taking up residence in this cell?' Officer Rice came to the cell door.

Red-faced, Kavanagh hurried out. Rice followed her.

'Well, what did she want?'

'Just a note written.' She showed the envelope.

'You know that's to go into the box for censoring?'

'Of course I do!'

'Give it to me. I'm going to the office. I'll put it in.' Rice took the note and went to the perspex office. Opening the envelope, she began to read.

Officer Paddy plodded onto the landing and wheezing, shouted, 'Winnie, school. Stacey, school. Mags, school.' The three went out the gate. 'Be good now and work hard, ladies.' He locked the gate and went into the office.

'Would you listen to this, from the new one, to Dommo of all people! "My darling love Dommo".'

Paddy put his hand over the letter. 'God help her! She'll learn soon enough, poor girl.'

Rice folded the note and threw it into the box for censoring.

'Gate. Gate.' Paddy waddled out and unlocked the iron-barred gate for Mags, who came running back in. 'Jasus I thought there'd be a toila out there. I'm burstin'!' She scurried to the toilet cubicle.

Fright stopped Mags' urgent flow and the blood drained from her face. Rosie had opened the swing door and stood before her with a long sliver of glass in her hand, a rag bound round the thick end. She put the jagged point up to Mags's face and placed a foot into the crotch of her knickers.

'I saw ya with that scumbag screw again. Grass! What was she quizzin' ya about?'

'Nothin'.'

'Nothin', me bollix!'

'Honest, Rosie, honest. Please.' Her whispering voice trembled. Rosie had the glass dagger to her skin; the slightest move from either of them and it would slice into Mags' cheek.

'If you fuckin' well as much as mention my name or antin' about me to any scumbag bucket, your pretty little

51

face will be cut ta ribbons. Ja hear me? Do ya?'

'I'm not a grass, honest Rosie.'

'What were ya rabbitin' about then?'

'She was just tellin' me about her fella an' all.'

'Yea? Tell me about the poor bastard.' She eased the pressure on the glass a fraction. 'Is he a cop?'

'No, no, he's a ... a... accountin'. His name's Paul, they have a place out in Lucan.'

'Ahh,' Rosie's voice was sickly sweet, 'isn't that nice for them, now isn't it? Just remember,' the tone was vicious again, 'what I told ya, ri'? We don't like grasses in here. Ya wide?'

'Ri'! Ri', Rosie, I know.'

'Ri', now ya can finish ya piss.' Grinning broadly, Rosie put the glass into an inside pocket and left the cubicle.

Mags pulled up her clothes as quickly as her trembling hands could manage and ran out of the toilet. Rosie was strutting, fat-arsed, down the landing.

Mags launched herself into the air and landed on Rosie's back, getting her in a stranglehold. Animal instinct said 'Kill. Kill now or be killed'. She squeezed the fat, blubbery throat with manic ferocity and they collapsed on the ground as Rosie's knees gave from under her.

When awareness returned, Mags was being held up against the wall by two officers. Grinning prisoners formed a semi-circle around them and Rosie was being led away, purple-faced and coughing. As soon as Mags came to her senses, she stopped struggling and Paddy let go of her.

'So we have a little fireball here have we?' Officer Rice was panting with the effort of having separated the prisoners and was holding Mags in an armlock.

Mags wrenched herself free of Rice's grip and pushed her away.

'Fuck off you!'

The officer picked up her cap and counted on splayed fingers. 'One, starting a riot; two, assaulting an officer; three, telling an officer to "fuck off". That's all your remission gone by my reckoning. You're for the governor when he comes in, madam. Now get out to school quick and learn to be a better educated criminal, or I'll have you thrown into the pad right now.'

Mags ran to the gate, leaned her head on the cold metal and wept loudly.

'Go on with you now, Margaret. Out to school and don't get up to any more mischief, like a good girleen.' Paddy opened the gate and Mags ran out.

You may, Dear Reader, be surprised to read that there is school available to the prisoners. I am, of course, in favour of education. In our society, education is the channel, the ladder, which provides access for everyone to the fruits of civilization. It is no coincidence that the ignorant fail to appreciate that education renders an otherwise unequitable system fair. Some among us may be born into more fortunate situations than others, but it is the wonderful educational system in this little country of ours which ensures that all with talent have a chance to rise in society. It is no exaggeration to say that, as a result of education being available to all, we live in a meritocracy, a country where those of us with talent rule.

Of course, the society needs constant fine-tuning. The knockers, the lazy, the downright degenerate can blame the 'system' or 'the powers that be' for their woes, but a good educational system proves the foolishness of such ranting. Schooling ensures that those with merit, no matter what their social background, can rise to positions of power and influence. It also ensures that the lazy will be free to wallow in their ignorance. As for those unfortunates who simply do not have the talent to prosper, well the blameless poor should not be held in contempt; there will always be tasks suitable for such people. The hidden hand of the market will work to the benefit of all. Prosperity inevitably trickles down.

I'm sorry if I have been long-winded in extolling the

virtues of education, but I did not want any reader to underestimate my appreciation of it. I would go as far as to say that, after religion, education is the greatest privilege that can be bestowed on the young. It is important to remember, however, that education is just that: a privilege – a privilege that one earns by hard work and diligence. And that is the reason why I believe that it is wrong to provide it, at great expense to the taxpayer, to those who have not earned the right to it. I ask you, do the victims of vicious assaults get compensated with free education? They do not! Yet the perpetrators of the same assaults are, while in prison, positively pampered with education provided in small groups which would be the envy of many a primary school teacher.

Take the case of a child abuser. Educationally mollycoddled in prison, to emerge a more articulate and plausible individual, he may be capable of finding employment in fields hitherto closed to him, such as the tourist industry, where he will have more access to children than he could have dreamt of before!

A little knowledge is, indeed, a dangerous thing. This very piece of writing proves my point. The author, almost certainly a product of the prison school, has in an attempt at literary style, and with simple-minded analysis, written a work of propaganda thinly disguised as a novel. Had she been the product of a deserved, appreciated and therefore proper education, she would not have written such drivel. But back to the text, because to any reasonable, educated reader, it illustrates my point exactly.

The school's great, Mags was thinking. How would she have survived this far without it? It was like being out of prison for a few hours each week. The teachers treated you like a human being and she was learning to read and write.

One month done and, as no charges had been brought relating to the fracas, three, or at the worst four, to go.

Monotony was the norm for Mags, but she had never experienced such depths of boredom. Sensory deprivation heightened her awareness. She lost herself in the cracks of the plastered cell wall. Odours related stories, changes in sound patterns outside the cell informed her of each officer's activities.

Every morning she woke up feeling that something was missing from her chest. Immediately she would remember her baby and calculate how long it was until the next visit when she could hold her again.

Her mother managed to bring the child up once a week. Between the cleaning job and looking after Tracy and her own baby, she was very busy. Mags knew it was not easy for her, but she wished she could see Tracy more often. She spent the half an hour just hugging her. Sometimes she thought it would be better if the baby wasn't brought at all, but later she craved the next reunion. After the visits she lay in the cell numbed with depression. Crying might have eased the pain, but she could not afford to show weakness.

Overcrowding in the prison had made it impossible for the officers to separate Mags and Rosie, but since the fight there had been no more trouble between them. Mags learned to give the impression of tough insensitivity to prisoners and officers alike. If she had not managed to act strongly at first, she could now. And, by Jasus, she would! She learned to shout a lot and to curse at every opportunity. There was even a walk, a sort of swagger, she copied from the long termers.

But Mags was not tough. She felt deeply depressed, lonely and frightened. For the next few months she would have to tread a fine line between giving the impression that she was tough enough to look after herself and not actually getting into trouble.

It's funny though, Mags thought, the worst things that had happened to her had led to the best things – like getting pregnant and then having Tracy. Now being sent to prison had led to meeting Dommo. They had a visit once a week, and even though they were separated by a partition and supervised by officers, they fell madly in love. She couldn't wait to get out and set up a new life with him. Christ, he was really gorgeous-looking! Sure there was no need to be depressed at all, she said to herself. A few more months and everything would be perfect.

'Rosie, visit,' Officer Kavanagh yelled into the recreation hall where a group of prisoners were watching the telly. Rosie had been glancing round towards the gate like a lion in a zoo near feeding-time. She got up and walked, as quickly as her tough image allowed, to the officer, who was waiting with handcuffs at the ready.

Mags turned from the telly and smirked. She could nearly feel sorry for Rosie, the way she had done herself up for the visit in a frilly white blouse and a short black dress that made the top of her legs look gross. The dress was belted in so tightly that she had two stomachs, like a camel's humps. As she walked unsteadily down the landing on huge high heels, the smell of cheap perfume wafted after her.

'I don't know where youse think I'm going to leg it to, going across the bleedin' yard an' out one gate. Sure there's still another six gates between me an' freedom. Do youse think I've learned ta fly, or wha'?'

'Rules, Rosie, rules.'

'Ah rules me bollix.'

She walked, chained to Officer Kavanagh, to a prefab building near the exercise yard. Inside was a long table, divided down the middle by a board standing eighteen inches high. At each end of the table sat an officer. Six women faced their visitors across it. Sitting on a chair you could see only the top of your visitor's head, so prisoners and visitors sat on the table.

'How ya, Garry?'

'How ya, love?'

Rosie sat on the table opposite a man with the good looks of a malicious Grecian god. His hair was swept severely back off his forehead in a black sheen. Although not tall, he seemed big. A boxer's physique bulged under an expensively cut suit. With his untroubled, bronzed face, he looked younger than Rosie's thirty-eight years.

'Fuckin' awful, that's how I am.' Her voice boomed above competing conversations. 'How do ya think I am in this bleedin' kip? I can't have a shit without them knowing all about it. I'm tellin' ya, I'll go crazy one a these days. The kids all ri'?'

'Game ball. They'll be up to see you soon, so they will.'

'I should fuckinwell hope so after all I've done for them!' Rosie suddenly cooled. 'How's Darren?'

'Expecting his re-trial any day. It's looking good but.'

'An' Joe?'

'Ja not hear? Got two year for possession with intent to supply.'

'No wonder there's nothin' but emigration and unemployment in the kip.' She glared at the officer at the end of the table, defying them to contradict her.

'Bleedin' right ya are, sure don't I know.'

Kavanagh joined an officer at one end of the bench and waited to escort Rosie back. She watched as the conversation between Garry and Rosie continued. Garry stretched over the partition and took Rosie's hand.

'No touching, please.'

'Jasus!' Rosie shouted. 'We haven't met for a bleedin' week an' we can't even hold hands. This place will be the fuckin' death a me, tellin' ya.'

Pointedly, Garry put his hand into his pocket. Kavanagh stared in disbelief as his fist went up and down, suggestively, in his trousers. Leering, he glared into the young officer's eyes.

'What's wrong, love? Ya never seen a fella scratch his balls before, or wha'?'

Officer Kavanagh blushed to the roots of her hair and looked quickly away. Garry's hand left his pocket and went to his mouth.

'Maybe she thinks you're playin' with yourself.

Wouldn't blame you if you were, poor thing.'

'Five minutes,' Kavanagh called out.

Rosie fixed her with a vicious look. 'That's ri', cut the visit short cos you're in a bad mood. That's lovely that is.'

'There's five more minutes of the regulation time left; it's nothing to do with me.' God, Kavanagh thought, will I ever be able for this job, when I can't even stop myself from blushing.

'Now come here to me, Garry, I've lots to tell ya. Tell that Mary one I'll kill her if I ever hear she's been mitchin' again, ri'?' He nodded. 'An' tell Paula that if I ever hear that she's seein' that whoremaster Jason, I'll have her guts for garters.' He nodded. 'An' give Christine a few bob for me. She'll need it for the first holy communion, ya wide? An' don't be bleedin' mean about it. She'll need a good few hundred. Give her eight, no give her a grand, ri'? She'll need it for the dress an' things.' The list of Rosie's directives seemed endless but eventually she was interrupted.

'Time up.'

'Gis another few minutes, for Jasus' sake!'

'I'm sorry, but time's up.'

'Here, come here to me, me poor love.' Rosie and Garry leaned across the partition and exchanged a lingering French kiss.

'Rosie, no physical contact, no touching! You know the rules. Stop that now!'

They broke apart and Rosie, eyes squinting to two malignant black slits, glared mutely at the officer.

'Ah leave it out, woman, will ya?' Garry's voice was conciliatory. 'Leave it out, sure there's rules an' rules in it, ya know?' He went to leave. 'Bye love,' he said. 'Don't worry about a thing, everything's under control. See ya next week. Ri'?'

Mascara was running down Rosie's face. She grunted as Garry left the prefab and waited without complaint while the young officer fumbled, trying to put the handcuffs on her.

'I'm sorry to have had to put an end to your visit, Rosie, but if I don't get back in time to bring another person out, they'll be late for their visit and I'll get into trouble.'

Rosie grunted.

'Do you understand my problem, Rosie?'

Rosie nodded.

Observing Rosie out of the corner of her eye, the officer was wondering if she was still crying and unable to answer or was the silent treatment part of her arsenal of abuse, when she saw her make a sudden movement of her free hand across her face. Kavanagh's heart began to pound. She knew what she should do, but had she the courage? She could pretend that she had seen nothing and avoid a lot of unpleasantness. She hesitated for a second only.

'Come this way, Rosie, please.' Rosie jerked back on the handcuffs, hurting her wrist and stopping her dead.

'Where the fuck ya goin' now?'

'Sorry, Rosie, but I'm calling for a search.'

She reached for the walkie-talkie strapped to her hip. As she gripped the radio, Rosie's free hand clamped her wrist, preventing her from lifting it.

'Listen you, poxface.' Rosie's voice was a threatening hiss, which made the novice officer's blood run cold. 'I know where your little loverboy Paul lives in his cosy little kip in Lucan. Ja hear me? I know all about him an' his fancy accountin' job. My associates inform me that he's a pretty little fella. Be a pity if he got hisself cut up, like, ya know?'

Kavanagh stood open-mouthed. Rosie yanked on the handcuffs and pulled the speechless officer along behind her. Back on the landing the officer's hands were shaking as she took off the handcuffs.

'That's a sensible girl now,' Rosie sneered. 'Any time you're thinkin' a makin' life difficult for me, just remember Paulie's furry little ballies. Ya wide?'

She swaggered down the landing, leaving the officer supporting herself against the wall. Stumbling into the prisoners' toilet and putting her hands over her face, the trembling young officer exploded into tears. 'Mags,' she said with venom, 'you dirty bitch you! How could you have done that on me?'

Calming herself with difficulty, she dabbed her eyes with cold water and walked out onto the landing with a new expression on her face. Her jaws were clamped and her eyes had an uncharacteristic squint.

Dinner was being served and Rosie went to the top of the queue to join Mags and Betty, who eyed her anxiously. They got their meals and were locked into the cell. As the key turned in the lock, Betty eyed Rosie's inscrutable face. Silence descended for a few seconds, then Rosie winked slowly and deliberately.

'Ya got it! Ya got it!' Betty exploded like a twelve-year-old. 'Thanks be to the lamb of divine Jasus! Blessin's a God on ya, Rosie.'

'Cool it.'

'OK, Rosie, OK.'

'How much ja owe me now, Betty?'

Betty's excitement evaporated instantly.

'Two grand, about.' Rosie opened her mouth to speak, but Betty interrupted her. 'Two an' a half, nearly. Y'all get it, so ya will. I'll have it to Garry within a month a gettin' out. Six weeks at the most. Ya know I can make that in no time arall on the canal.'

Rosie glared at Betty. 'Do I but? That's what I'm wonderin'.'

'Wha' are you insinuatin' ...' she began to shout, but thinking better of it, controlled her temper and tried to ignore the insult. 'Ah Rosie, what ja mean be tha'?'

'What I mean is that if ya come back in here without havin' paid in full, I'll do for ya. That's what I mean.'

'Ya don't have ta worry; s'no problem to me, so it's not.' Tears welled in her eyes.

Mags' heart went out to her, she looked so pathetic.

'Get the door,' Rosie barked, and Betty jumped up and put her back to the spyhole. Having beaten a tattoo on the pipe and got a satisfactory reply, Rosie took a plum-sized ball wrapped in clingfilm from her pocket. Betty went to have a close look at the heroin.

'Get back, ya fuckin' gobshite ya.'

Betty jumped back.

Taking a razor blade from the padded cover of the Bible, Rosie crushed a small mound of powder onto the table and, using the blade, divided it into minute amounts which she wrapped in clingfilm.

'Cut off a teenchy little bit extra for me, Rosie, love, will ya? Sometimes it does be cut up worse than meself like.'

'Don't you ever,' Rosie was vicious, 'don't you ever accuse me of cheatin'. I'm a respectable businesswoman an' I'll have no fuckin' junky accuse me of cheatin'. Not even you, ja hear?'

'Jasus, t'was only jokin', Rosie, honest I was. Sure ya know that, Rosie!'

'You're a dirty fuckin' drug-pusher,' Mags was surprised to hear herself shouting, 'that's what ya are!' She had been determined to keep away from anything that might get her into trouble, but now she found herself on her feet shouting at Rosie. 'Respectable businesswoman me arse!'

'I never asked no one ta take drugs in me life, so I didn't.' Rosie pointed the razor at Mags like a swordswoman. 'So just don't start or I'll sort ya out this time. Ja hear me?'

'Ya don't scare me, so ya don't,' Mags lied, as her eyes swept the cell for a weapon. She hadn't thought before she had shouted, but it was too late to back down now.

Betty threw herself between them. 'In the name a Jasus, the screws will be here in a minute an' we'll all end up in the black hole. Please!'

Rosie knew she was right. If there was a fight and the screws caught her with bits of gear all around the cell, she was in serious trouble. Mags too realised how stupid she had been. She sat down slowly. Rosie handed a heroin sweetie, about a quarter the size of a pea, to Betty, who snapped at it, like a starving dog at a piece of meat from its owner's hand. Ripping a sanitary towel, Betty placed the little package inside the padding and the towel inside her knickers. 'It's gas. I use hundreds a these an' I haven't had me flowers for years.'

Rosie put several of her 'sweets', along with the razor, into the padded cover of the Bible.

Mags lay on her bunk with her hands behind her head. She pretended disinterest, but watched out of the corner of her eye, with a mixture of fascination and disgust, as Rosie took down her tracksuit bottoms and pants, inserted two fingers deep inside her body and pulled out a condom. Putting the plum-sized package of heroin into the condom on top of the four tablets already there, she reinserted the bulging rubber.

Closing her eyes, Mags prayed silently for safe delivery out of this hellhole.

Her clothes back up, Rosie wriggled her lower body until she seemed satisfied. Betty left the spyhole and, pulling her bunk underneath the window with an ear-splitting shriek of metal on concrete, climbed up on the top mattress.

'Ay, Snake!' she shouted through the bars, broken glass and mesh.

'Wha'?' a despondent voice drawled.

'It's a fuckin' great night, isn't it?'

After a pause the same voice answered, from closer, it seemed to Mags. 'What ja say?'

'I said it's a great fuckin' night, so it is. Stars all over the bleedin' kip.'

'Great, yea,' came the voice, animated now.

'Tell him stars don't grow on trees.' Rosie stood with her back to the door.

'Stars don't grow on bleedin' trees, ya know.'

'I know, I know. I have it well covered, honest.'

Rosie left the door, got the hairbrush, and beat a tattoo on the pipe. The beat echoed from cell to cell. Rosie went back to the door and silence descended.

Betty put her arm between the bars and through one of the broken glass squares, stretching until it hurt. Eventually, with the concentration of an eye surgeon, she drew in a delicate string, at the end of which was a small plastic bag. Landing her precious catch, she mumbled an incantation, untied the bag and shouted out the window. 'G'night, Snake.' The string disappeared. Betty emptied the contents of the bag onto her lap. A blackened spoon, a dirty medical syringe, a needle and some bluetack rolled out. The syringe was cracked down the length of the barrel and had been crudely doctored with some of the bluetack. The plunger was worn too small for the barrel and had paper wrapped around it to help it function. The needle was bent almost into an S.

Trying to occupy her mind with something else, Mags took a school copybook from under her bunk and attempted to decipher the marks the teacher had helped her put there. She knew that the letters made up words like dog, cat, rat and mat but right now she could not concentrate. Betty was putting the works together and Mags' eyes were drawn to the procedure.

Betty tried to screw the needle into the syringe, but the thread was worn and it flopped from side to side until she moulded bluetack around the joint. She tried the plunger. Not satisfied, she wound another piece of paper around the worn washer.

Mags made another attempt to read.

'Hurry up with the works for fuck's sake, will ya?' Rosie was getting agitated. She took her back from the door and put her ear to it. 'Come on, the screws will be back on their rounds any minute. Hurry.'

'Ri', ri', hold ya bleedin' horses.' Betty's voice shook. She couldn't get the plunger into the barrel. When she eventually got the bockety equipment together, she put it on the floor under the bunk where it lay in the overflow from the pisspot.

Arranging the spoon so that it stuck out over the side of

the table, Betty used the Bible to weigh down the handle. She put the specks of heroin onto the spoon and poured a few drops of water over it from a plastic bottle. Her hands were shaking now just like Mags had seen her stepfather's hands the morning after a heavy drinking bout. She struck a match, held it under the spoon and melted the drug; it turned the water murky. Perspiration dripped from her nose as she took the plunger out of the barrel, poured in the thick cloudy liquid and returned the plunger without spilling a drop, despite the terrible shake that now seemed to be affecting her whole body.

'Hurry, will ya for fuck's sake?'

Betty did not seem to hear Rosie or see Mags throw her copybook against the wall in frustration.

'Ya not afraid of the virus?' Mags asked Betty.

'Would ya not mind ya own business, would ya not?' Betty snapped.

'But sure ya know half a them have it, don't ya?'

'Leave it out, Mags.' Aggression sounded through the shake in Betty's voice. 'Mind ya own bleedin business. It's my bleedin' life, if ya want to call it a life arall.'

'Get fuckingwell on with it,' Rosie commanded from the door.

Taking off her tracksuit bottoms, Betty made a tourniquet with a pair of tights which she squeezed around the top of her right leg. She aimed the syringe at the back of her knee. After a few seconds, she placed it on the floor again and with both hands, squeezed the tights around her skinny, abscess-covered leg. 'Well Jasus fuck it inanyway! Me awl reliable has collapsed.' She repeated the procedure with the tights on the left leg but to no avail.

'Hurry, I said!' Rosie was becoming exasperated.

Taking down her knickers, Betty sat and scrutinised her groin. The look of her, naked from the waist down, except for her knickers around her spindly, white and scabrous legs, revolted Mags, but her eyes were glued to the obscene ritual.

Betty took the works back up from the dirty floor and pointed the needle into her pubic hair, deep in her groin. Sweat gathered in the wrinkles of her face as she made several attempts to push the blunt and twisted needle into her artery. With every attempt, she squeezed her eyes shut and whimpered painfully. 'Jasus, this fuckin' needle's as blunt as me bollix. Twista it is.' She jabbed the syringe viciously.

Loud sighs of pleasure signalled her success. She stretched her arms as if in adoration, as a quiver enveloped her body, the empty syringe dangling between her legs.

'Goddd! Oh Goddddd!'

She relaxed, smiling confidently, her face transformed, vibrant and pretty.

'Won't be a minute now,' she said cheerfully and, taking the syringe in hand, she pumped the plunger slowly and sensually, filling the grimy barrel with anaemic blood each time. As watery plasma trickled from the crack in the syringe, Betty's eyes sparkled.

Mags jumped off the bunk and grabbed for a pisspot. Too late, she vomited all over the floor.

'Ah Jasus, ya poor little love ya! What's wrong? Sure it doesn't hurt arall, so it doesn't. I just had ta flush a few times to make sure I got it all.' Mags was still retching. 'Ah ya poor thing ya. Ya all ri'?' Relaxed and self-confident, Betty had taken the syringe out and had dressed again. She held Mags around the shoulders to support her.

'Ah for fuck's sake!' Rosie held her nose, as the smell of vomit filled the cell. 'Here,' she continued, 'get the works out a here quick. Ja hear me? Quick!'

As Betty was disassembling the syringe, a tapping was heard on the pipe. Keys jingled outside the door.

'Jasus! Jasus!' Rosie went into a panic.

As the door was about to be opened, Betty moved with cool efficiency, sweeping the plastic bag under her pillow and lying down on the bunk. Kavanagh swung the door open.

'Uh!' She fanned the air in front of her face. 'What has happened here?'

'Ya wan,' Rosie nodded towards Mags. 'It's the shit yis serve up for dinner. Has her poisoned, so it has.'

'Indeed. Anyway yourself and Betty are for the social worker.'

'Wha'? The social worker at this hour?'

'Yes. We can't all sleep our lives away, you know. Now hurry.' She moved down the landing away from the stink.

'Gis a chance ta put me runners on, will ya?' Rosie shouted, then whispered to Betty, 'Stall her for a minute.'

Betty sauntered out as Rosie, whispering urgently to Mags, took a piece of heroin from its hiding place.

'Listen, as quick as ya can, put that inta the plastic bag with the works, ri'? The string is down, get it an' tie the bag onto it an' shout to Snake antin about the stars. Ri'? Ya'll have ta hold it and stick your arm as far out as ya can, otherwise the string will break an' we're all in the shit.'

Mags stared into Rosie's fat-encased eyes. 'Ya mean *you're* all in the shit.'

'Listen, just get rid of it quick, will ya?'

'Come on, Rosie,' Betty shouted, just before the officer stood framed in the door again.

Carefully avoiding the mess on the floor, Rosie joined Betty and they walked down the landing towards the gate.

Mags picked up the half-full pisspot which had vomit splashed on its side and went to walk out past Officer Kavanagh. 'Can I empty this an' get stuff to clean up the mess?'

The officer blocked her way. 'Can I empty this,' she spoke very slowly, 'an' get stuff to clean up the mess, please, officer?'

Mags' brow wrinkled in confusion. 'Can I empty this an' get stuff to clean up the mess, please?'

'Officer.'

'Officer. An' I need sometin' ta settle me stomach, please.'

'It's not only your stomach that's sick. You can live with it till morning, and serves you right, you bad bitch you!' She slammed the door with a force that made Mags' ears ring.

The confused prisoner stared at the door for a few seconds and as the stink of vomit filled her nose again, she started pounding the metal. 'Ya poxy scumbag ya. Yer all the same, so yis are, a shower a bastard buckets.'

Muffled by the heavy door, the obscenities followed the officer as she walked back down the landing. She did not have to hear the exact words to get the message. She was learning to cope with the abuse by disengaging totally. Gone were all her foolish ideas of giving and getting fair play, of earning respect by showing kindness. Prisoners, as Officer Rice had said, were too far gone; she could see that now – they were beyond redemption and could not respond to such niceties. Having been stabbed in the back by Mags after all her kindness to her, she knew that Rice was right. She was happy now that she had asserted herself, shown that she could be tough. Yes, I can survive in this godforsaken place, she thought, her hands clenched into white-knuckled fists. I'll have to toughen up fast, but I will survive. I won't be driven out by some low-life scum of the earth.

Banging the door and shouting at the top of her voice tired Mags out quickly in the putrid air. She went straight from screaming abuse to crying like a baby. Collapsing on the bunk, she sobbed, trying to figure out what was happening to her, but the more she tried to make sense of things, the more her head spun. She had not believed the prisoners when they told her that all the officers were scum. Now she could see that they were right. The one officer who had been nice to her had been winding her up to stab her in the back.

'Fuck yis all. I'll never fall inta that trap again,' she cried out. She thought of the love letters she and Dommo had exchanged and blushed to think of the officers sniggering behind her back at what they had both written. Bastards.

The smell of vomit was going to make her sick again.

She mopped it up with a toilet roll as best she could. Getting up on the bunk under the window, she pushed the paper out through the bars and broken glass. She noticed the string hanging outside and wondered if she should help the others at all. Fuck Rosie, she thought, but decided to get rid of the gear for Betty's sake. Anyway she wouldn't give the screws the satisfaction of catching anyone. She couldn't think with the smell.

Taking a bottle of cheap perfume belonging to Rosie, she sprayed it around the cell. She wasn't sure which was worse, the perfume or the vomit.

Her head was spinning as she got the plastic bag from under the pillow and climbed back onto the top bunk. Craning her neck around to see if the coast was clear, she could see little of the dark yard below.

'Snake?'

'Who the fuck's that?'

'Mags.'

'What jew want?'

'Isn't the stars beautiful?'

'Oh yea, ri', nice one, fair play to ya.'

'Hold on a minute.' Stretching out, she could not grab the string. She had to lie down on the bunk and jam her head and shoulders against the bars, but eventually managed to get it. Taking a last look around the dark yard, she tied the bag to the string and held it out as far as she could. 'The stars is smashin'.'

As the bag was drawn up, Officer Rice walked around a corner of the yard. She stopped and stared.

'Ay!' a confused voice shouted from Snake's cell window, 'what about the bleedin' stars? What kind of a wind-up is this? Hay you, Mags, the bleedin' stars.' The bag arrived down again.

It took her confused brain a few seconds to realise what Snake was talking about, then it clicked. Putting her hand into her pocket, she felt the clingfilm containing the drug which she was supposed to have sent up with the works.

Meanwhile, Officer Rice ran from the yard, shouting into her radio for reinforcements.

Stretching out to retrieve the bag, Mags had the side of her head and her shoulder pressed against the bars, but a breeze was blowing the light plastic just out of her reach. It spun as the tips of her fingers touched it.

Six female officers scrambled around the perspex office, following Rice's call for help.

'Help me with this, quick.'

'Zip me up, hurry.'

'Dirty bitch, I knew she was a bad one.'

'Hurry or it will be gone.'

'Where are the bloody batons?'

'Right come on now quick, but keep it quiet.'

Six officers strode down the landing. Three were dressed from head to toe in heavy, white plastic space suits, white helmets covered their heads and came down to their shoulders, with only a small visor for their eyes. Wearing 'durex' gloves and white wellingtons, they looked like scientists in a cheap horror movie. The other three wore ordinary riot gear, heavy black coats over bulky protective padding, head and face cocooned in black helmets. Long batons in hand, the six strode down the landing like opposing teams in some outlandish American ball game.

Mags' fingers pinched a corner of the bag and she drew it carefully in. Sitting with her legs over the bunk's edge, she perched on one cheek of her bottom. She stretched out her leg and fished in her trouser pocket for the package.

The cell door crashed open. Mags shrieked in terror at the sight of the ferocious black and white monsters charging into the cell.

'We know –' a muffled voice screamed before Mags' foot shot up instinctively and caught the foremost creature under the chin, sending it sprawling backwards. A white monster jumped, and grabbing Mags by the foot, dragged her off the bunk. She avoided hitting her head off the ground by grasping the thing around its neck but her hands were wrenched from her support and she fell to the ground screaming. Terrified, Mags kicked and punched wildly as she writhed on the floor. The cell was packed with weird shouting figures. She felt something get a hold of her feet and drag her along the vomit-lubricated floor.

Prisoners started to scream abuse from their cells. A pisspot was pounded off a metal door and the prison erupted in a frenzied din, as all the prisoners joined in.

White foam bubbled from Mags' mouth with the force of her terror. All went dark. She was rolled over and over and her arms and legs were firmly bound.

Blinded, she felt herself being transported through the air. Lack of oxygen stopped her screaming but the prison was bedlam, the noise reverberating around her panic-stricken brain. Falling as if from a great height, she hit the ground with a thud and began to spin as in some nightmare merry-go-round. She saw the light again, as a riot clad officer rolled her out of the blanket which had bound her. A door slammed shut and the ranting from the cells was silenced.

'Right, hand it over!' Standing above her, surrounded by strange beings, was Rice. The officer was deathly pale and trembling. Bloody mucus oozed from one nostril.

Incapable of speech, Mags lay there, her body heaving with open-mouthed, silent sobs. Riot head-gear was removed, revealing the human form of Mags' attackers. 'Hand it over, I said. We know you have it.' Rice turned to the other officers. 'Search the cell. Don't let the other occupants back in till it's fully checked. Now, Margaret, hand over the drugs and save yourself a very unpleasant search.'

'Drugs? What drugs? I don't use drugs. I haven't any,' Mags bawled, so disorientated by the sudden and unprovoked attack that she did not make the connection between it and any drugs. Now, however, her predicament dawned on her. The realisation that she did have heroin sent terror up her spine.

'Lying will only make matters worse, Margaret. We know exactly where ye hide them and we'll retrieve them if we have to. This is your last chance. Hand them over, now!'

'I've nuttin', nuttin', I swear.'

The door of the padded cell opened, letting the pandemonium from the other cells flood in. The two officers arrived back and, stepping on to the soft floor, closed out the mayhem again. 'It's clean, nothing there,' one of them reported.

'Just as I thought,' Rice shouted above Mags' protestations. 'Right, strip her.'

The officers hesitated, each waiting for the other to act, their country faces showing disgust for the job in hand. Pressing herself against the padded wall, Mags made fists of her hands and bared her chattering teeth.

'Now, Margaret, more aggression will only make matters worse. Look, we have a nightdress here. Take off all your garments and put it on. If we are satisfied, the search will go no further.'

Mags kept her defensive rigidity, her teeth still chattering, her face deathly white. Helmets were replaced and four officers rushed at Mags, who kicked and punched, making no impact on the heavily padded suits. In an instant she was pinned to the floor, clumsy gloved hands pulling off her clothes. Her shrieking gave way to wailing and pleading.

'No, no stop, fuck off, please, no don't, I have me flowers, I have me flowers, pleassse. I want me mammy, I want me mammy!'

A gloved hand was placed over Mags' frothing mouth. Two young male officers, reinforcements sent because of the emergency, arrived panting and pushed in the heavy door as the female officers had successfully removed Mags' clothes. Standing behind Officer Rice, they watched the struggle, grins broadening on their flushed young faces. In the confusion it took some seconds for anyone to notice their arrival. When it dawned on Rice, she took each by the arm and guided them firmly out the door. 'We have the situation well under control now. Ye may go back to your normal duties, thank you.'

By now Mags was rolled into a tight ball in the corner of the padded cell, one arm clamped between her legs, the other hiding her face, her body shaking uncontrollably. The searchers were going through her clothes like gorillas looking for mites.

The twisted piece of paper was discovered and opened to expose its venomous white kernel.

'Look what we've found in your pocket.' Pushing the drug up to Mags' face, Rice sounded vicious. 'I want me mammy,' she mimicked, 'I'm only a poor little drug pusher,' she continued slow and threatening. 'Right, we want the rest. We know where you have it. Give it over or we'll have to take it.'

Each riot-clad officer stared at Rice, searching her face for evidence that she was bluffing. They looked horrified. Rice was white and shaking, her skin taut around her mouth. To their disbelief, each concluded that she meant what she said. They were still staring at their colleague when Mags' blood-bloated tampon hit her in the face.

I am sorry, Dear Reader, to be exposing you to this gross writing, but as I warned, there will be a good measure of such ugliness before we have finished our quest. This is a good point at which to bring to your attention the misguided, if not downright stupid, ideology which underpins the thinking of those who drove me out of my position of influence.

You will remember that I subscribe to the theory known as the Classical School of Criminology. This, to recap, holds to the idea of justice as an exact scale of punishments for equal acts, without reference to the nature of the individual involved, or the circumstances under which the act was committed. Private property is held in high regard and the means of gaining property is regulated by law. Of course, rationality is denied to the criminal action.

My detractors subscribe to a more modern school of thought – the Positive School of Criminology. They see themselves as being involved in a Copernican-like revolution in matters of justice. Just as Copernicus proved that the earth was an orb revolving around the sun, and was suppressed and ridiculed by the powers of his day for his trouble, so the Positivists would have us think that their ideas are simply misunderstood by an ignorant establishment. They feel confident that in time they will be proved to have turned one hundred years of enlightened and disciplined study on its foolish head. So let us cast a fair if critical eye on their criminological version of *On the Revolution of the Celestial Orbs*.

The Positivist criminologists see their role as the elimination of what they consider to be the 'metaphysics' of the free will of the classical school and its replacement by a science of society. (We are back, to the 'determinism' nonsense I referred to earlier.) They wish to replace the notion of free will with a science of society. Seeing their job as the elimination of crime, they are not interested in philosophy or in ethics. These modern-day Copernicans insist on the unity of the sciences – that is, that the scientific method of nature has equal validity for the study of society. They assert the law-governed nature of human actions and wish to develop accurate and calculable units of crime and deviance. It follows from their assertion that deviance should be dealt with scientifically, that it is subject to discoverable causal laws. They assert that the criminal automatically reveals himself by his actions and is propelled by forces of which he himself is unaware. Social life, they insist, should be explained not by the notions of those who participate in it, but by more profound causes which are unperceived by consciousness. Juries therefore, should be replaced by panels of experts, punishment by therapy.

So, being scientists, our friends the positivists must

73

develop scientific laws. To test the metal of their ideas, we shall look at one of the most famous of these: Ferrie's Law of Criminal Saturation. This states:

> Just as in a given volume of water at a given temperature, we find the solution of a fixed quantity of any chemical substance, not an atom more or less, so in a given social environment, in certain defined physical conditions of the individual, we find the commission of a fixed number of crimes.

So Positivism holds that human behaviour must have the quality of things; it focuses on the criminal actor, not on the act. It is a doctrine of non-responsibility for actions and is opposed to punishment.

Really, Dear Reader, need I go on? In my defence of a more traditional and commonsensical approach to crime and punishment, could my argument be made any stronger than by giving the newfangled ideas space to hang themselves? I could rest my case here, but instead will refer you back to the text of this abominable document which vindicates my position beyond doubt.

To and fro, to and fro, Mags rocked on the floor of the padded cell, chin on chest, arms hugging her knees to her body. She wore only a filthy nightdress. A grey blanket and a filthy pisspot were the only objects in the small, square, windowless room. Dingy grey light came reluctantly from a single bulb, buried deep in mesh on the ceiling. The padded walls and floor were heavily stained with shit and blood. The smell and absolute silence oppressed her brain. Hate born of frustration was her only stimulus and she drew on this in full measure, learning an appreciation of its bitter-sweet poison.

How long had she been in the 'black hole', she wondered? A week, a month? In lucid moments she concluded that it was all a nightmare and she would wake up soon with her baby snuggled warm and cosy beside her in her own clean bed! For most of this eternity, however, her mind turned in and cannibalised itself in a hateful entanglement of demented impressions.

Every couple of days, by her own estimation, the door was opened, cleaning equipment and disinfectant put in and she was ordered to clean the pad. When she did not respond, food was placed on the floor and the door closed. But she had just sat there rocking. The door had slammed each time and left her to the smell of her own body wastes.

Mags jumped up screaming and ran from wall to wall, crashing into them, kicking and punching. Then, exhausted but unhurt, she went back to rocking. She slept fitfully. Was it night now, or was it day? Was her baby all right? Was her mother alive or dead?

Why, she wondered, were they torturing her like this? Why did they beat her up and humiliate her? She had done nothing wrong; she had obeyed every rule, but the bastard screws had deliberately provoked her and set her up for a beating and the black hole.

OK, she had agreed to send the drug up, but as far as she knew, she was the only one in the prison who was not taking drugs. Anyone could see plainly that there were drugs everywhere. Sure, didn't the screws give them out three times a day to anyone who wanted them? Why did she, the only one in the whole gaff who didn't take them, get the beatin'? Well they would soon see, so they would. If they thought they could get their rocks off by pickin' on her, they had another thing comin'. She could be as tough as them any day.

Trying to figure things out made her head throb. A new defiance crystallised in her disorientated brain, a rebelliousness against screws and cops, pigs and rats. Jasus, she'd show them, the slimebags. She grabbed the pisspot and threw it against a wall. The silent explosion sent shit flying to the four corners of the padded cage.

Days (or was it weeks?) passed. The door was opened

and again Mags did not give them the satisfaction of bothering to look up. She felt a gloved hand take each of her arms. Two officers lifted her and walked her towards the door.

'You're for a shower now, young lady, and then back to your cell.'

She pushed their hands away aggressively and walked unsteadily between them to the shower cubicle.

Absence of prisoners on the landing suggested that it was night-time. She threw off the shit-stained nightdress and showered without closing the diminutive doors.

'I survived, I survived!' she said to herself as the rejuvenating water washed away shit, sweat, and menstrual blood. The frugal comfort of feeling clean again made her want to cry with relief, but she was determined to show no emotions to the screws.

The flow of hot water was cut off and Kavanagh came into the cubicle with a towel and a clean nightdress.

'Dry off now and back to your cell.'

Mags, wet and naked, stood up close to the young officer, snatching the towel from her hands.

'Does your little accountant know that his slut is a secret dike what gets her rocks off by watching women having showers?'

The officer's face betrayed only the slightest hint of her revulsion. 'Back to your cell now.' She hoped she sounded unperturbed.

Mags put on the nightdress and made her way to her old cell. Only Betty was there. Nothing was said until the door was slammed, but Betty's face registered shock. Mags had lost weight, was deathly pale and had thick black rings around her eyes. A hard expression had replaced her childish look of innocence.

Betty jumped up and went to Mags, who had sat on the bunk with her back rigidly straight, eyes betraying no emotion.

'Mags, ya poor love ya. Ya all ri'?' Betty took her in her arms and Mags collapsed into her embrace in hot tears.

'Ah sure god help ya! Sure I know how ya feel, ya poor little thing ya!' Betty rocked her and rubbed her back as if Mags was a baby with wind. Eventually she became calmed enough to speak.

'How long was I in there?'

'Three days.'

'Three fuckin' days? Leave it out, will ya. Three fuckin' year ya mean.'

'Not windin ya up love, three days, honest.'

'Jasus fuckin' Christ, that all? Well if they think I fuckinwell care, they have another thing comin'. Scumbags!' She blew her nose and wiped her eyes. 'Where's Rosie?'

'Moved her to another cell. I think they're on ta her. Inanyway, I have a good supply so I do, so fuck them. That reminds me: I have a little present for ya, make ya feel much better, so it will.' Betty took an orange from the table and, squeezing it, opened a gash in its skin. From this she fished out a small, foil-wrapped parcel. 'Look,' she held up a chunk of dope, 'I'll make us up a nice big joint. Would ya like that?'

'Nice one, Betty. I'll pay ya back when I get outa this kip,' Mags said in her new hard tone.

'Notarall.'

Betty rolled the joint expertly. Drawing on the fat joint herself several times, she silently handed it on. Mags sucked on it like a greedy child, the soporific fumes soaking deep into her lungs.

She had only tried to smoke dope once before and had caused her friends to scream laughing at her attempt to keep the smoke in her lungs. The sensation she had experienced was nausea. Now with all the roll-ups she had been smoking, it was no bother to keep the smoke down.

'Jasus that's great stuff,' Mags said, exhaling reluctantly and, sucking another intake of dope into her lungs, she handed the joint back to Betty, who had been staring at it anxiously.

As Betty smoked, a wonderful feeling of calm came over Mags. Lying on the bunk with her hands behind her head, she drifted into a serene state of mind. The tension and hatred of the last three days dissipated. Betty handed her back the small butt and she managed to get two hungry drags out of it before the taste of burnt cardboard invaded her throat. She coughed, then jammed her hand over her mouth to save the precious dope from escaping a second too soon.

Betty exploded into a fit of laughing and billowed out smoke before she too put a hand over her mouth. She pointed to Mags and they both, with hands over their mouths like wise monkeys, rolled around in silent convulsions of mirth, until it was all just too funny and they burst out in loud guffaws. Mags hooted and giggled until her ribs hurt. Tears of hilarity rolled down her cheeks.

The pain in her ribs was really severe. She fought hard to stop laughing, but every time she looked at Betty they went into fits of giggles again. Eventually the laughter ebbed and she managed to take a deep breath.

Thick lazy ropes of blue swirling smoke filled the cell. Mags gaped at the beautiful designs it made in the bars of light from the window and marvelled at the gracefulness of the slow-motion coils of aquamarine.

Betty slid off her bunk and, waving her arms about sluggishly, executed, as Mags perceived it, a graceful ballet dance, as she tried to disperse the incriminating art display. 'Jasus,' she drawled as she danced, 'we'd better get rid of the bleedin' smoke, else we'll both be in the fuckin' pad.'

The futility of Betty's attempt, when what she was doing was making the designs swirl all the more ostentatiously, caused Mags to burst into laughter and sent Betty into hysterics again.

If a screw came to the spyhole, there would be trouble, Mags knew, but nothing bothered her. The more she tried to stop laughing, the more she laughed. Turning to the wall, she covered her head with a pillow.

When eventually she got control of herself, Mags felt wonderful. It was as if she had been massaged all over: all the tensions were gone, all the hurts and pains.

She lay on the bed thinking and everything became clear to her. The muddled fears and emotions of her life were now understandable; she could see where she had been going wrong, although why it had taken so long to see what was now so obvious she didn't know. It was not for want of her friends telling her. 'Jasus, Mags,' they would say, 'you're too up-tight, so ya are. Go with the flow a bit will ya, for fuck's sake? Ya don't smoke, ya never get drunk, reckon ya've only had one good shag in ya life. Would ya ever relax an' live a bit?'

They were right; she could see that now. All her stupid worrying about her mother, worrying about Tracy, about getting a job, about learning to be a cook, worrying, worrying and never just relaxing and enjoying life. Yes! She would just have to learn not to be so up-tight from now on.

Now that she thought about it, it was her stupid ambition that had led her into prison even. Hand-me-down clothes were not good enough for her baby, oh no! She had to go out and get the very best. She was even too stuck-up to accept presents of baby clothes from her own mother. Anyway, things would be more relaxed now; she would live with Dommo and have a far better life.

Dommo! She looked over to Betty, who seemed to have fallen asleep. Dragging her bunk to the end wall, she climbed up on it. 'Dommo,' she shouted out the window, 'ja miss me?'

'He got out, Mags,' Betty drawled, her eyes still shut. 'Yesterday, sudden like. He didn't expect it for a couple a more months. Overcrowdin'!'

'Ay,' a strange male voice shouted from a distant window, 'I missed ya awful, so I did.'

'Fuck you.' Mags jumped down from the springs. 'Jasus, that's great,' she said unconvincingly.

Suddenly, Betty became as excited as a little girl in a sweet shop. 'He sent ya down a pressie but!' She held out a clingfilm package. 'Jasus!' she giggled, 'he must be cracked about ya altogether. There's enough here for a couple a bleedin' months.'

Stunned, Mags took the gift. Somehow she knew without asking; it was heroin. She gawked at it open-mouthed.

Betty broke the silence. 'Oh yea, an' he said to tell ya that he'd get ever'tin' set up outside and he would visit ya as soon as he could. An', and, oh yea, not ta worry about a thing, an, ah, oh ya, not ta let them wind ya up cos it would only give them an excuse to fuck ya back inta the black hole. An' ah, what else d'say now? Oh yea, he says he loves ya, an' that when ya get out ever'tin' will be great, cos he loves ya an' he'll look after yourself an' the snapper.'

Betty looked pleased with herself for having memorised everything so well. She beamed at Mags. 'Can I have a little bit, love,' she beseeched. 'I kept it safe for ya last night.' She paused. 'Well only used a teenchy bit, like, ya know?'

'Wha'? Oh yea, yea sure.' Mags shook her head as if she was waking from sleep. 'Better hurry though or them scumbags will have me back in the black hole.' The venom was back in her voice.

Betty scrambled up on the springs.

'Ah Snake, ja love me or wha'?'

'Ya must be bleedin' jokin', ya ugly awl bag ya.'

'Bollix to you too, ya slimy awl Snake ya.' Betty had an air of confidence about her. 'All the same, it's a great night but.' She paused for effect. 'Wha' with the stars an' all, like?'

A frantic banging erupted on the pipe. Betty jumped down as Mags hid the drug under her pillow. The key sounded in the lock and Officer Rice and Officer Paddy stood into the cell. They started a search.

'Ya lookin' for another excuse to beat the shit outa me, ha?' Mags asked and stood in Rice's way.

'Beat *you* up? That's a laugh. If you hadn't resisted, there would have been no trouble at all. As it is, there's one of my officers out recovering from injuries you inflicted on her and I have two loosened teeth after your assault.'

Paddy was conducting the search half-heartedly. As he was about to lift Mags' pillow, she sat down on it.

'Too good for yis,' she sneered at Rice. Paddy searched elsewhere, mumbling to himself. Rice waved a threatening finger at Mags. 'That's two assaults on officers and possession of heroin. Very serious offences. The governor will decide what additional charges are to be brought.'

''T'was yous that attacked me, yis shower a –'

'You are in no position to get stroppy, madam, unless you have anything to tell us which might make life easier for you.'

'I'm no bleedin' grass. Ya can go an' fuck off, so ya can.'

'Now just you behave yourself or you could see a lot more of the pad in the near future.'

Paddy finished his fumbling search and the two officers left the cell.

'Jasus, Mags, that was a close one.'

'Fuck them anyway, scumbags!'

'Jasus, the works!' Betty scampered back up on the springs and hauled in the string. It had a blackened spoon tied to it. 'The dirty bollix, he wants the deal first, so he does.' She got the blade from its hiding place. 'Here, gis it. I'll cut it for ya.'

'I'll do it meself.'

Taking the heroin from under the pillow, Mags divided off three small amounts as Betty guarded the spyhole and advised on quantities. 'Ri', that's a deal for Snake, one for his cellmate an' ya own bit, Betty. How much is each a them worth ja reckon?'

''Bout thirty pound each, Mags.'

'Christ almighty. That means me stash is worth about four, five hundred pound?'

'More. Six hundred, easy.'

Mags wrapped the precious crumbs and sent them up on the string, having checked carefully for a presence in the yard.

'Tellin' ya, Mags, he must be cracked about ya altogether

to give ya a pressie like that!'

Betty paced the cell waiting for the works to arrive.

'How much ja use in a day about, Betty?'

'Sixty pound worth, when I can get it. More when I'm outside. Before I came in this time I was usin' about three hundred a day.'

'Jaassus!'

'Yea Jasus! I know, mad isn't it? They're great in here but, they give ya Phy if ya strung out. Only thing is, it's more addictive than heroin. An' the medics always give me uppers after I cut meself.' Betty looked down at her multi-coloured arms. 'Shitloads sometimes, dependin' on who's on duty. They don't last me long but. Still dey kept me floatin' through many's a day.'

'How ja get all the money ya owe to Rosie an them? Ya must be great at dippin'!'

'I'm not inta dippin arall!' Betty was indignant. 'I earn it down the canal.'

'Wha'? Jasus!' Mags's brow wrinkled, but she went on sympathetically, 'That must be awful, Betty.'

'Ah no. Sure it's all ri'.'

'Lettin' any awl bastard do ya?'

'A sure most a dems very nice, really, very clean an' considerate like.'

After a short silence, Mags' curiosity overcame her disgust. 'How much ja charge?'

'Depends. I used ta get really fancy money.' Betty's shoulders slumped and the fun went out of her eyes, 'Charge less now but. It's a bleedin' disgrace so it is, the dismissive society has business ruined. Most fuckers are gettin' it free these days. Five pound for a hand job, ten pound for the business, an' fifteen if there's any extras. Some of them would give ya more than ya'd ask for. The priests is the best but. Christian charity, I suppose.'

'Priests?'

'Yea priests. Ya get lots a them so ya do, that's what syphilisation has got to. They wear civvies, but ya can smell

82

the incest offa them. Ya know? Like at mass. This priest used
to bring me back to his kip; Jasus yad want ta see it, huge, so
it was. He musta been mad, there was books all over the
bleedin' kip, an' no telly, no video, nuttin'! But inanyway, he
used to pay me three hundred pound, so he did. For nuttin'
special like, just a double barrel. Ah yad have to pity him,
poor bastard!'

'A double wha'?'

'Double barrel! That's when they want to come twice
like, ya know?'

Mags nodded, hoping that her revulsion was not
obvious, as Betty carried on enthusiastically. 'Jasus it would
burn the hole offa ya, the way they take so long the second
time. Three hundred pound. Massive wasn't it?'

'Sure!' Mags fought back the bile of her disgust.

'Jasus, Mags, you'd be able to charge a fortune. Make a
bleedin' mint, so ya would.'

'No thanks.' The very idea made her want to vomit.

'Really Mags yad –'

'Leave it out Betty. Ri'?'

She was saved from wounding Betty's feelings by a loud
voice singing out of tune, 'Don't let the stars get in your
eyes, don't let the muan break your heart.'

'Jasus, the works!'

Betty scrambled frantically on to the bunk. She pulled in
the delicate string, and unsheathed the contents of the
plastic bag. She put the narcotic on the flame-blackened
spoon. Lacking water, she filled it with white lemonade.
Holding her cigarette lighter under it, she cooked until the
heroin dissolved into the sugary liquid, then with shaking
hands, emptied it into the syringe. Mags faced the spyhole
as Betty took down her pants and injected the needle into her
groin. Sounds like sexual ecstasy announced the completion
of the task. Mags gave her time to arrange her clothing, then,
looking around, told her to hide the syringe.

'I'll have to give it back as quick as I can, Mags.'

Betty was about to put the syringe into the plastic bag

but then hesitated and asked casually, 'Ya goin' to try a little yourself, Mags, seen's it's your pressie from Dommo?'

Tranquillised by the hash, Mags felt relaxed and self-confident. It was easier to figure things out in this pleasant state. They had told her that hash would turn her into a raving lunatic, but she never felt better. And who were 'they'? Straights, like the screws, sadistic bastards with power, who wanted to control and oppress. Screws, police, priests, all in their uniforms of brutality, telling her to do this, do that, don't do this, don't do that. Something that made you feel as kind and loving as hash did couldn't be the evil 'they' made it out to be. It was 'they' who could do with loosening up, to learn to live and let live. They were the ones who did the battering and belittling. A little dope would do them a power a good!

Dommo had been her lifeline since she had come into prison. Without his love, she felt she could not have survived. All her life it seemed as though there had been something missing, something she yearned for. Sometimes she felt that she was on the verge of understanding what the missing element was, the thing which, if found, would make her complete, a real person, not the confused ball of needs and insecurities that she had been. Dommo, she felt sure, was that thing! When she got out of this hell-hole, she would live with him and be whole. She loved and wanted Dommo and if a little heroin was good enough for him, it was good enough for her!

'They' had forbidden this fruit, to force people to live in ignorance of the good things in life and she would not abide by their prohibition, she would not live in the visible darkness of oppressive 'straight' society.

Like Dommo, there was no way she would ever use it often, just a little now and again to help her through the torment of prison. Obviously, that's what he had wanted; to give her a little something to get her through. Dommo wasn't an addict – he was too clever to get himself hooked. God, but it was good of him to give her such an expensive present – it showed how much he loved her.

'Mags?'

'Wha'?'

'I said, ya havin' some yourself?'

'Fuckin' ri' I am. It's mine isn't it?'

'Course it is, Mags. Nice one, love.'

'Will you get it ready for me? Just a small bit.'

'Course. Just enough for a nice little hit, OK?'

Preparing the fix speedily, Betty talked Mags through the various procedures.

When the fix was ready, she handed it to Mags, who took it with a mixture of fear and awe. The soporific affect of the hash had her senses dulled beyond caring. Still, she could not bring herself to stick the twisted needle into her flesh.

'Will ya do it for me, Betty, please?'

'Sure, course I will, love. Look, this is how ya do it. 'Seasy really, doesn't hurt, just like a little pinch. This spike's blunt but. It's hard to get them in here. I mean I wouldn't put a six-inch needle up me, so I wouldn't! You wouldn't neither, wouldn't ya not?' Giggling, Betty wound a pair of tights around the top of Mags' arm, causing a half grape of blue vein to pop up. Mags looked away.

The pain was awful as Betty jabbed several times. Mags was about to pull her arm away and tell Betty to forget it when her guts filled with the most beautiful warm creamy sensation.

The hole in Mags' chest was filled. She had been a lost child wandering in fear. Now she was home. There was no more suffering, no more sorrow. All was happiness and joy, every pore of her body throbbed with pleasure. She simply was; and being was wonderful. She was bliss.

Betty glided gracefully around the cell, having returned the works. Mags realised how much she loved this kind creature who was the very embodiment of sweetness and light.

'Ya OK, Betty love?'

'Brillo, never better in me whole life! You?'

'Smashin'! Let's do sometin. Ya still got ya tattooin' gear?'

'Yea sure. Why?'

'I want me borstal spot, just like yours. An' a "I love Dommo" here.' Mags opened her tracksuit and bra and indicated her left breast. As Betty stared at her breasts, Mags saw them herself as if for the first time. They looked wonderful to her, perfectly proportioned instruments of nourishment. Remembering that she had not breast-fed Tracy because she considered it disgusting, she marvelled at how beautiful it would have been. She would have a baby for Dommo, she told herself, and breast feed it until it was big and healthy.

'Put the radio on, Mags, an we'll have some music while I do your tattoos.'

Mags switched on and as Betty prepared her equipment, the sounds of a chorus flooded the cell with the most beautiful sounds she had ever heard.

Betty wound thread around the point of a needle and forced it into the ink container of a biro.

'Ri', Mags love, sit here on the floor between me knees an' I'll do the borstal mark first.' Betty, black-tipped needle in one hand, put the other at the back of Mags' head and jabbed the needle repeatedly into the unblemished flesh of the kneeling teenager. Each stab sent a delicious electric shock through Mags, who could not stop swaying her head to the music.

'Hold steady, love, will ya, or I'll make a ri' dog's diddy of it.' Betty renewed the ink on the needle.

Mags felt secure in the warmth between Betty's knees. She closed her eyes and drifted with the stars, every pleasurable jab of the needle in harmony with the music.

'OK, love, that's that one. We can go over it again another time if we have to. Now, "I love Dommo", ri'?'

'Ri.'

'That will take a good bit longer, but sure we're not goin'

nowhere in a hurry, are we?'

Mags felt Betty cup her breast in her warm hand. A tingle fluttered through each breast, met in the middle of her chest and trickled down her stomach to an exquisite explosion between her legs.

As the music melted to an end, Betty finished the tattoo. Mags had no idea of how long it had taken; she didn't care. A voice on the radio announced more music, something about a handle and a chorus performed in the fields. She got a fit of the giggles, imagining an evening-suited orchestra and choir performing in a muddy field, surrounded by attentive cows and sheep. The lights went out.

'Only just finished in time, hah? Didn't think it was that late?'

The sudden blackness was illuminated by bright bars of silver slanting from window to floor, as the voices of a thousand angels filled the cell. Still kneeling between Betty's knees, Mags felt her naked breasts being soflty massaged and little explosions tingle all over her ultra-sensitive skin. Her heart swelled to a heavenly chorus of 'Unto us a child is born'. Standing on tiptoe, her thigh muscles stretched in expectation, she felt her trousers being slid down and Betty's hot urgent breath between her thighs. Hands slid from her breasts, brushed down her sides and warm fingers kneaded her bottom. She wriggled with delirium as Betty's wet tongue found her little cleavage with its minute pink pearl and washed it in butterfly strokes of ecstasy. A taut spring snapped between her legs, uncoiling in tissue-tingling spasms of pleasure.

Betty stood and slipped off Mags' remaining clothes. She stepped out of the garments and, stripping Betty, explored the sensuous braille of her body with slow, intense interest.

Mags followed Betty's warmth into the bed where they lay entwined in gentle embrace. Betty massaged Mags' back and she responded in kind, copying every little touch as magical fingers brushed her back and then her neck, her breasts, her stomach. The spring was wound again to unbearable tension. Her body became a tingling mass of sensations.

'God, you're so beautiful Mags; you're fabulous!' she heard whispered, as the music soared to the heavens. 'Wonderful! Marvellous!' Betty ran her hand gently between Mags' knees and up near the top of her thighs, massaging slowly. She urgently wanted to grab Betty's hand and place it at the very source. Instead, she brought her own hand between Betty's legs to her secret place. Betty responded and spasms of pleasure convulsed them.

Mags was falling and there was nothing to fear, the more she fell, the more intense her pleasure. 'Jasus, Jasus, Jassuuuss!,' she cried. 'Hallelujah,' celestial voices sang, as she fell, pleasure enveloping her in an impenetrable cocoon of happiness.

It may come as a shock to you, Dear Reader, to discover that drugs are so easily available in Irish prisons, but unfortunately it is the case. The text is accurate on this point, as indeed it is on most aspects of prison life. What makes this manuscript dangerous is the slant that is given to the facts of prison life. However, the issue of drugs in prison is most important.

Now my detractors, the feminist, 'prison as holiday camp' lobby, want it both ways. They pressured me into having as lax security arrangements as possible, and at the same time used me as a scapegoat for the inevitable failings of that regime. And one of the adverse results is the ready availability of drugs.

When the drug problem first began to manifest itself, I recommended a series of stringent security measures. Being well aware of the type of women we were dealing with, I recommended to the minister such measures as body searches and a week of isolation for all new prisoners, to foil attempts to smuggle drugs in on their person; glass partitions with intercoms, to eliminate all contact during visits; and an end to temporary release, for funerals or sickness.

'Fascist.' That is how my recommendations were described in the media, and the minister declined to implement them, for reasons of political expediency. Or, as I am now free to say, because he did not have the courage of his convictions, and would rather ensure his own re-election than safeguard lives.

Then, my brave armchair criminologists used the availability of drugs in prison as a stick to beat me with. Ah, the hurler on the ditch! I am sure you can imagine the frustration when, in my case, the hurlers were allowed to jump off the ditch and assault me with the hurleys, claiming that it was a stick of my own making! I am guilty of wanting a fascist regime when I recommend proper drug-excluding measures, and I am guilty of incompetence when the prison is swamped with drugs, because I am not allowed to implement these very measures!

Typically, my detractors are incapable of distinguishing between a sensible regard for law, order and tradition, which is called conservatism, and an unchristian, radical form of collectivism, which is fascism. And if they have problems with my drawing on common sense and tradition, what of their politics? They are, no doubt, liberals. Unlike the English who, were lured by the simplicity of liberal ideology, the Irish were protected from such foolishness by their attachment to the land. Happily, liberalism's day is over. On these islands, however, there is still one last bastion of this discredited ideology. I speak, of course, of Dublin 4, from where (strange coincidence!) most of my critics hail.

So what is the liberal position on drugs in society? What would my critics bring about if they (God help us all!) were in positions of power?

They advocate a policy of laissez-faire. That is, they advocate doing nothing! They would have us believe that drug-taking is a private matter and that governments should have nothing to do with it. If one woman wants to buy heroin and another wants to sell it to her, they claim that that is a free exchange of services and the women are perfectly within their rights. As with alcohol, they say, so with heroin, hashish, and any of these abominable substances. What the individual does in private is his or her own business and is no concern of government.

And what if that woman becomes addicted, and ends up selling her body on the streets to support the addiction? Well, our great ideologists say that this also is no concern of government. If a man wants to buy sexual favours, and a woman wants to sell them, this is a free exchange of services.

And if the addicted person takes to beating old women over the head, to steal money for their drugs? I would like to have the opportunity of asking my opponents that question!

Drug-taking and prostitution they describe as 'victimless crimes'; and where there is no victim, they hold that there should be no crime. In the actual exchange of drugs or of sex for cash, neither party to the transaction makes a complaint and, as a result it is very hard to enforce laws relating to these activities. From these facts, they conclude that there should be no attempt to enforce such laws, that the activities should be decriminalised. Legislating for private conduct, they say, amounts to making laws that reflect a particular moral code, and forcing this morality on the populace. They insist that the law has no place in the private domain. Because the powers that be both use and make money from alcohol, the argument goes, it is deemed to be moral and therefore legal. Since those in power neither use nor profit from heroin, they consider it immoral and illegal. In what they consider to be an amusing phrase, they describe leglislating for victimless crimes as an attempt to encase Ireland in a chastity belt.

I am no prude and have no difficulty in saying that the working man is entitled to his pint. Being a moderate drinker, I might be accused of prejudice, but to confuse alcohol and drugs is, to my mind, sheer stupidity.

And what is wrong with legislating for a particular

morality? Our moral code in Ireland is based on Christian ethics – the guiding principles in every civilised country for two thousand years. Are we to give these up, at the behest of a handful of educated dunces?

What these people forget is that private morality affects the public domain. Even if the addict was not driven to acts of public outrage (which he is), his immorality sets a bad example and contributes to a decline in public standards. Where the hedonistic philosophy of unlimited personal gratification has prevailed, as in the dying days of the Roman empire, honesty and virtue declined and society perished in a cesspool of vice. We see in the spread of AIDS God's punishment, his way of bringing home the message that abusive behaviour is detrimental to both body and soul.

The ideas of the Liberal, secular-society clique should not be dignified with a debate, for fear that those of weak mind might be influenced. The work under review shows the inevitable outcome of these dangerous ideas.

'Well, wha' ya think?' Dommo pushed the door open with his foot. He was carrying Mags, who was herself holding Tracy asleep in her arms. The misshapen borstal mark stood out against the flush of excitement on her face, as he carried them into the one-roomed flat.

'It's only gorgeous. I love it, Dommo.' She kissed him.

Dommo ran back down the flights of dirty stairs to get the pushchair, as Mags looked around the bed-sitting-room with its beautyboard walls, minute kitchen space, and the area where the bed, with its yellow-rose cover, stood. There was a tubular-metal table and four plastic chairs. Two old armchairs faced an electric fire in the tiled fireplace. On the mantelpiece, a Spanish dancer in crimson skirts swirled in plastic glory. In a corner, under the high ceiling, was a baby's cot. Frilly-pink drapes formed an arch over it.

A guilty feeling that it was not as nice as her little house had been crept over Mags; yet in another way, this was better. This was their place. And, besides, Dommo would not hear of her keeping the house on. He was going to provide them with a home and that was that!

He arrived back up with the pushchair.

'It's a bit small for the three of us, Mags,' he said, 'but the rent's not bad arall. Inanyway, I have plans. In no time arall we'll have a huge big kip all of our very own.'

'Plans! What plans?'

'Don't you worry your pretty little head! Plans that's all.'

'Where did the smashin' cot come from?'

'A present for you an' Tracy.'

'Ah Jasus, Dommo, ya shouldn'ta! Jasus, it musta cost a bomb.'

'Never mind about the price; nuttin's too good for you an' our Tracy.'

Mags placed the sleeping child in the cot. 'Ah but Dommo, ya shouldn'ta.' She gave him a hug. 'I'm not even a day out an' ya have me spoilt rottin, so ya have.'

'Ja like the room but?'

'Love it, Dommo, an' I love you.' She ran her hands over his short bristly hair. He was not tall but he had worked out regularly while he had been inside, and he was fit and strong. She thought he had lost some weight since he had left the prison, but still he was looking good.

This, she thought, was the first day of her real life, the life of happiness she had always longed for. She would make Dommo the happiest man on earth.

Tracy made a gurgling noise in her cot and Mags rushed over to her, but the baby was sound asleep.

'Ja know what, Mags? She's goin' ta be the spittin' image of ya.' Dommo looked at the child with genuine affection. 'She's goin' to be fuckin' beautiful. When she wakes up, can I feed her, Mags?'

'Course, let her be now but, I don't want her woken, after the way she screamed when we collected her. Didn't even know me, the poor little thing. An' me poor ma bawlin' her eyes 'cause I was taken her.'

'Your step-da didn't look sorry ta say goodbye, did he? Didn't seem to like me neither.'

'Fuck him. If he did like ya, I'd be worried, so I would.'

'Listen Mags, I'm bleedin' starvin', are you?'

'Yer! I could eat the hind leg offa the lamb a God, so I could. I'll go to the shop.'

'No way, not on ya first day out, inanyway. I'll go the curry shop meself, an' get a Chinese.'

'Can we afford that, Dommo?'

'I told ya not to worry. Money's gonna be no problem.'

'Ri', Dommo, that's great. We'll be able to eat in peace before Tracy wakes up. That reminds me, while you're out, will ya get nappies, an' a few jars a chicken baby food?'

'Sure. What ja want at the curry shop?'

'Whatever you're havin' yourself.'

'Chicken curry an' chips, then.'

'Great.'

Dommo was halfway down the stairs when she shouted after him. 'Will ya get twenty smokes, Dommo?'

Mags looked around the room. It was great, she thought: no smell of chamber pots, no bars on the window. Best of all, no screws orderin' her about. However, she could not convince herself of this. She expected, at any moment, to hear the key turn and the door to burst open and a big uniformed culchie to barge in. Going to the door, she opened and closed it several times, half in disbelief that she possessed the power to do so. She sat down. Her happiness was tinged by the fact that she was feeling a bit fragile and tense.

She and Betty had had a party in the cell with the last of her present from Dommo, to celebrate her impending release. Mags had to admit that she had taken a lot of heroin by her own standards. It was, though, the last turn-on she would ever have! She had taken heroin every night since she had got the present, but only a small amount. Well, just enough for a little treat, and to get her through the long nights.

Now that she was out, there would be no more of that!

She would be a wife and mother. No more drugs, ever!

She had a cold coming on, which was why she felt a bit under the weather. Her bones were sore, and she had a headache. If Dommo had any hash, she might have a smoke. But nothing else!

She turned on the electric fire to take the chill out of the air. It would be awful if she got a flu on her first night out, she thought, especially seeing as she was looking forward so much to getting into bed with Dommo. That would be her substitute for the nightly turn-on. Dommo was the fix she really wanted.

Sex reminded her of sleeping with Betty, but that had not been sex. She had been so embarrassed waking up beside her that first morning, but Betty had explained it all to her. It was something nearly all women had to do in prison, to keep themselves from going crazy. It didn't mean that they were dikes or anything. They were just keeping each other warm until they got out to their men again. Dikes did all sorts of disgusting things to one another with dildos and stuff like that. All she and Betty ever did was caress and cuddle. It was funny, though, Mags thought, Betty's caresses gave her some wonderful feelings all the same. Usually though, they both went to sleep after a turn-on, without knowing what, if any, bed they were in, and caring less.

She was beginning to wonder what was keeping Dommo, when she heard footsteps on the stairs. Screws, she thought, coming to raid the cell! She shivered.

Dommo opened the door and walked into the room beaming from ear to ear.

'Surprise, surprise!' He was followed by a man and a young woman. All three were laden down with bags. The smell of curry might have reminded Mags of how hungry she was, but the surprise of seeing familiar faces from the prison made her forget her hunger.

'Ah Jasus, Tina! Nice one!' Not only did Mags know Tina from the prison, but she also recognised Rosie's husband Garry from the visiting box. 'When ja get out?'

'Just after yourself. Overcrowdin', so they gave me temporary release, to go to me sister's weddin'.'

'Brillo! Which a them is gettin' married?'

'None a them, as far as I know inanyway. The screws don't know that but!'

Dommo was removing steaming cartons from plastic bags. He seemed a bit on edge. Curry smells competed with the smell of hot vinegar.

'Ah yous! Will yis stop the rabbitin', an' let me introduce Garry to me woman, in the name a Jasus!'

Garry's build made Dommo look small and insecure. Mags reckoned that he was the spitting image of the man in the ad for pizzas on television, but she averted her gaze from his dark-brown eyes, and felt herself go puce with embarrassment. His stare made her feel naked. He was really handsome, but he was married to Rosie, and too old to be with a seventeen-year-old like Tina. He must be nearly thirty-five, Mags thought.

'Mags,' Dommo said nervously, 'this is ...'

Garry stepped up to Mags, putting out his hand.

'Hi! I'm Garry. I'm very pleased to meet you, Mags,' he said in a deep voice, stressing 'you' in a way that made Mags feel sort of special. She thought her face was about to burn up with embarrassment as Garry pumped her arm slowly and scrutinised her face. 'Ja know what it is, Dommo? You're a very lucky man so you are!' He was still gripping Mags' hand. She stared at the bright green lino. 'No doubt about it, she's a very beautiful woman, very beautiful indeed.'

At the word 'woman', Mags' head shot up, and her eyes met his for a second before she looked back to the floor. She had never been called a woman before, nor had thought of herself as one. She was confused, but sort of proud as well.

'Sure don't I know! She's me little princess.'

Dommo was embarrassed too. He put a proprietorial arm around Mags. 'Wait till yis see the kid,' he continued, 'another bleedin' beaut!'

Garry and Tina lavished praise on the sleeping baby.

Every word was like nectar to Mags, and she began to feel a bit more relaxed.

'Anyway, grub.' Dommo rubbed his hands. 'I don't know about the rest of yis, but I'm bleedin' starvin' so I am.' He put the electric kettle on and started to empty the contents of the cartons onto plates. Bright-yellow curry sauce was poured into raths of white rice, and loaded with greasy chips for himself and Mags. Garry and Tina sat down to chicken balls submerged in congealed, psychedelic-pink sauce.

From a bag, Garry produced bottles of whiskey, vodka and red lemonade, 'to celebrate Mags' release'.

'A Jasus,' Mags ventured her first words to Garry, 'ya shouldenta, Garry, so ya shouldenta.'

'No bother, Mags. Any friend a Dommo's is a friend a mine.' Without asking, he poured large measures of vodka into cups, and handed them to Tina and Mags. Pouring whiskey for himself and Dommo, he held his cup up over the table of steaming food, brown bags and silverfoil containers. 'To Mags and Dommo.'

'Nice one. Fair play ta ya, Gar,' Dommo said. 'You're the best mate a guy could have.'

Garry kept his cup outstretched. Hoping his response was appropriate, Dommo bumped his cup clumsily off Garry's. The girls followed his example, giggling. 'Nice one, Garry,' they mumbled in unison.

Mags nearly choked, trying to suppress a cough which would spray the table with booze. Even though she had put lots of lemonade into her cup, she gagged as the hot liquid shot up her nose, bringing tears to her eyes. When the vodka hit her empty stomach, she felt instantly hungry, and began shovelling up the bright yellow substance.

'It's all right, isn't it? That's not a bad take-away around the corner, all the same, isn't it not?'

'Not bad at all, Dommo. Fair play ta ya.'

Dommo was relieved by Garry's endorsement.

Tina's face was flushed with the booze which she was knocking back at a great rate. 'Curry's great with the vodka, isn't it, Mags?'

Mouth full, Mags nodded agreement.

Garry aimed a gold-ringed finger at Tina. 'Bleedin' chisler's drink, so it is.' Nobody contradicted him. He finished eating, grated back his chair, stretched his legs, lit a cigarette, and blew a cloud of smoke over the table. 'I like a woman,' he said staring at Mags, 'who can do bird, an' take no shit from the screws.' His brow wrinkled, and his piercing eyes narrowed, as he turned to Dommo. 'Course it should never happened! No woman should ever have to do antin' what might land her in the clink. Ya know what I mean?'

Dommo attempted to gulp down a mouthful of curried chips in order to answer, but Garry went on, leaving him pop-eyed, and choking on the acidic mess. 'Any man what lets his woman do crime is only a bollix. It's men's work, and only men's work. Some guys have no pride any more, no principles arall. Lettin' their women go out an' earn their livin' for them! Jasus, what's the world comin' to?'

Dommo managed to swallow. 'Gar, I didn't even know Mags when she got nicked.'

'I'm not sayin' ya did, Dommo. Don't get ya knickers in a twist. I'm just sayin' a woman's place is in the home, that's all. Ya know what I mean?'

'Yer, Gar!' I'm always sayin' so meself. It's no business for a woman.'

Garry's probing eyes alighted on Mags again. 'Still, I have to say, Mags, fair play to ya! Heard all about the grief the screws gave ya. Ya've been through the mill, an' you're one of our own now, so ya are.' Lifting his cup in salute, he winked knowingly at Mags, and took another swig of whiskey.

Non-plussed, Mags drank the vodka, without taking the time to add lemonade. Proud to be praised by Garry, she was afraid she might cry and make a complete fool of herself.

Dommo broke the awkward silence. 'Nice one, Gar.'

Tina and Mags cleared the table, and started on the washing-up. Filling everyone's cup again, Garry went to the women at the sink, and led them to the chairs facing the electric fire. 'That can wait till later! Come on, knock back your drinks and have another.

The girls didn't dream of refusing Garry, whose eyes were sweeping the room.

'Ya any tapes to go with that yoke there, Dommo?'

He pointed to a ghetto-blaster.

'Sure, Gar. What ya into?' Dommo took tapes out of the food cupboard. 'Ya inta The Progeny, Gar?'

'The who?'

'Haven't got them.'

'Haven't got what?'

'The Who.'

'Ya haven't got the who?'

'No.'

'No what, in the name a Jasus?' Garry shouted, his eyes glistening under a heavy brow.

'No, ha-ha-Who, Gar. Ya know, The Who, ga-Gar.' Dommo was stuttering like a weak pupil answering a Christian Brother.

'Jasus Christ, I don't know what you're on, with your ha ha whoin', an' your ga ga Garin, but it's doin' ya fuckin' head in so it is, an' mine as well, I can tell ya!' Garry grabbed the tapes from Dommo's hands, sending several clattering across the lino. 'In the name a Jasus, have ya nothin' we can dance to?'

'Dance? Sure Gar, sure.' Dommo picked up one of the tapes and timidly offered it for Garry's approval. 'What ja think a this one, Gar?'

'I said dance,' Garry shouted, frowning dismissively at the tape, 'ya know like? Dance? Not jump around the kip, filled to the gills with ecstasy, like a frenzied lunatic with a red hot poker up his arse.' He chuckled. The other three laughed loudly, eyeing Garry carefully. The tension eased. 'Real music Dommo, rock an' roll, me awl flower.'

'Jays, Gar, I'm not sure. Maybe this one?' Dommo put a tape into the ghetto-blaster and pressed the button. The room exploded with discordant electric shrieks, and the ranting of strife-filled voices.

Garry jumped out of his chair. 'Jasus fucking Christ.' He slammed down the off button, restoring quiet. The baby grumbled in her cot, and Mags went to her. Garry took a set of keys from his pocket, and threw them to Tina. 'Nip down to the car, for Jasus' sake, and get some real music like a good girl.'

Tina hurried out, unsteady on her high heels. Mags rocked the baby back to sleep, as Garry refilled the cups.

When she arrived back Tina's face looked almost healthy from having rushed down and up as quickly as her shoes would allow. 'These what ya want Gar?' She scrutinised his expression as he checked the tapes.

'Just the job, love.' He patted her on the bottom, and she went back to her chair, beaming.

No sooner was Tina sitting than Garry grabbed her by the hand, and pulled her out of the chair, as Elvis Presley's voice howled from the ghetto-blaster.

'Come on, dance. You two as well, come on.'

Jiving expertly, Garry slid around the lino in perfect time with the music. Tina partnered him awkwardly on her stilettos. Mags gyrated dutifully opposite Dommo, worrying that the loud music would wake the baby. Her flu was getting worse, and she wished she could just give Tracy her night feed, and collapse into bed. Her head was throbbing from the booze and the effort to socialise after all those months living in a cramped box. Her back ached.

'Ah for Jasus' sake, can nobody dance any more? Jasus, what's wrong with yis anyway?' Garry barked, plonking himself down in a chair. The others were relieved to do the same.

'It's just that we're not inta the buzz yet, Gar, ya know what I mean? Not really wound up like,' Dommo said in a jittery voice that Mags had never heard before. 'I've just the number to liven us but!' Dommo went to a loose floorboard, and taking it up, produced a syringe and a minute amount of white powder. 'This will get us rockin', so it will.'

Garry shook his head with a look of deep disgust. 'For

Christ's sake, what's wrong with the kids today? Can yis not have an awl laugh an' a dance without pumpin' that shit up your arms? This is the only fix I'm inta, as ya know,' he said, holing up his glass and mellowing into fatherly tones. 'Suppose I'm just old-fashioned. Anyway if ya have ta, if ya really have ta, this party's on me.' He threw a small neat package of heroin into Dommo's lap, whose eyes dilated in excitement.

'Nice one, Gar,' he simpered. 'You're a real mate, so ya are.' He turned to Mags. 'Didn't I tell ya he's the greatest mate a guy could have, didn't I?' He was already getting the fix ready.

Mags smiled at Garry through a splitting headache. 'You're very good, Garry, so ya are. Ya shouldenta.'

The flu symptoms had weakened her resolve. What with feeling brutal, and the mortification of trying to act normal after four months inside, she was in rag order. A turn-on would be just the job. She would quit tomorrow. Anyway, it would be ignorant to refuse a present. Knocking back a gulp of straight vodka, she looked anxiously beyond Garry to where Dommo and Tina were shooting up.

When her turn came, she was about to shoot up when Garry shouted. 'Don't do that disgusting stuff in front of me, you! If ya have to do it,' he waved a hitch-hiker's thumb over his shoulder, 'do it outa my sight!' Mags scurried behind him. Before injecting, she hesitated, and was about to run the syringe under the tap, when it dawned on her how insulting it would be to Dommo and Tina. She injected deep into a vein, just as a fabulous piece of music came on the tape.

'One, two three o'clock,' boomed out. Mags just had to get up and dance. The music was great, and life was wonderful. Nobody noticed the baby crying, as they all began to jive. Garry grabbed Mags, and they moved like a couple who had been together for years. She loved every minute of it, feeling that the drum beat had a direct connection to her heart, as Garry twirled and turned her, and she responded to the slightest movement of his fingertips. She was graceful and athletic. 'Jasus,' she shouted above the music, 'Elvis is only smashin', so he is!'

'Bill Haley, ya gobshite ya.' Garry laughed, and Mags howled with mirth at her mistake. Mags wanted the music to go on forever.

But it didn't, and the baby's urgent cries filled the silence.

'Look after Tracy, will ya Dommo?' Mags ran to the ghetto blaster and stabbing at the buttons, managed to fast-forward to another lively number. Dommo put the baby on its stomach, and jerked the cot to and fro till the music blasted out. Then he went back to dancing. Tracy's high-pitched wail resumed, and competed, urgently with the bellowing music.

As Garry and Tina danced, Mags and Dommo cavorted with reckless abandon, sliding, twisting and turning. She jumped, entwining her legs around his waist, and as he held her wrists, let herself fall back. Dommo spun her around, her hair sweeping the ground.

Towards the end of the number, Garry sat down, pulling Tina onto his lap. When the music stopped, Tracy's cries filled the room.

'Right, folks, time to go. Get the coats, Tina.'

'Ahhhh Jasus, Gar! Sure the night's young. It's only eight a bleedin' clock, for Jasus' sake!'

'Sorry, Dommo,' he replied, 'but I still have business to attend to tonight.'

'Better get a bottle for me little princess,' Mags said, skipping across the room. She yanked the fridge open and, fumbling, knocked a carton of milk to the floor. Laughing, she managed to retrieve it while there was still some left. 'Fuck it anyway,' she giggled, throwing a tea towel into the pool of milk. Glassy-eyed, she checked the remaining milk. 'That much will have ta do; it's all there is in the bleedin' kip.' She splashed it ino a saucepan. 'Shrup you. I'm bleedin' comin', ri'?' She waved a threatening finger at Tracy, as the baby's distress increased.

Tina seemed reluctant to leave, but she went up to Mags to say goodbye.

Dommo sidled up to Garry. 'Listen Gar, talkin' a business, I have a good few contacts again now, an' like I could do with a deal. Ya know what I mean, Gar?'

'Ya know I hate doin business with users, don't ya, Dommo? Anyway ya have the two of ya to feed now, and the snapper. This is no time for to be startin' up a business.'

'I'm wide, Gar. Honest, Gar, I know what ya mean, but I just need to deal a bit for a while. I have this great plan, Gar.'

Garry frowned. 'It would want to be a fuckin' great plan altogether, what with your record an' all! How much ja owe me, Dominick?'

'Er, about a grand, Gar.'

'One thousand, four hundred, exactly.'

'Oh yea, I remember now Gar. One thousand four hundred pound, Gar. Ya don't have to worry but. I have it all figured out. I have this great stroke lined up, a dead cert. It's –'

'Listen!' Grasping Dommo's shoulder, Garry stared ferret-like into his pupils. 'I'm under big pressure from me business associates, Dominick, so don't let there be any fuck-ups! Ri?' He handed over a package. 'That makes it a straight two.'

'Nice one, Gar. Fair play ta ya!' Sweat glistened on Dommo's brow, but he had escaped the hypnotic stare. 'You're the best pal a guy could –'

'Two grand.'

'Ri', Gar.'

'Full payment in two weeks.'

'Jasus! Two weeks, Gar? Like the old bill is on me bleedin' back an' ...' Garry, one hand still on Dommo's shoulder, extended the other towards the package.

'Two weeks. No problem, Gar. Two weeks on the button.'

Releasing his grip, Garry went to the girls, who were chattering above the din of the baby's cries, as Mags poured boiling milk into a stained plastic bottle. Garry handed Mags a twenty pound note. 'Get the kid a present, love.' He nodded towards the door. 'Tina.'

Before Mags could respond, Garry had left, Tina jogging behind him. 'Two weeks,' she heard him say as he disappeared.

Dommo hid the drug, as Mags took the screaming baby in her arms, and stuck the dirty teat into its mouth. A moment's silence was followed by an unmerciful scream. Squirting milk onto the back of her own hand, Mags scalded herself. She went to the sink and plopped the bottle into water as the baby screeched in pain. The cooled milk pacified Tracy somewhat. She sucked greedily on the teat.

'Jasus, Dommo, isn't Garry only smashin' all the same? Looka what he gave to Tracy.' She held up the note.

'Least he could do, the dirtbird, after all I done for him.' Whipping the note from Mags' hand, Dommo shoved it into his pocket. 'Two fuckin' weeks, me bollix! Thinks he's big when Rosie's not around. She cuts him down to size. Wears his balls on her charm braclet, so she does.'

'Garry, a dirtbird?' Mags looked confused.

With the rush of heroin cascading through Mags' veins, however, worry was impossible. Dommo must have been joking, she concluded. Garry was a great new mate to have. Still in the first flushes of the hit, however, she was incapable of concetrating on anything for more than a moment. She sat the baby, still sucking on the bottle, in its cot.

Dommo grabbed Mags around the waist and moved his body against hers. His face betrayed no memory of worries, as for a moment their two sets of glassy, pinprick-pupiled eyes met, and each saw worlds within worlds, an infinity of fathomless universes.

'Ay com'ere. We're not in the visitin' box now. Touchin's allowed, Mags, ri'? Jasus, your only gorgeous but.' His hands massaged her back urgently, lingering half a tantalising second on her bottom.

'Dommo, ja know wha'?'

'Wha?'

'Jail was worth every bleedin' minute just to meet you.' She pulled his body to her, loving the warmth. His knee was between her legs, and the gentle pressure felt divine. 'Com'ere, look , I've a little sometin' to show ya,' she said breathlessly, unbuttoning her blouse with jittery fingers.

'Call them little?' Laughing, he cupped her ample breasts in his hands.

'Wait till I show ya, will ya?'

They giggled like conspiring infants, as Mags opened her bra, and Dommo struggled to focus on the 'I love Dommo' tattoo. He kissed the tattoo, and then the erect nipple. 'Fuck me, Mags, it's bleedin' beautiful,' he said reverentially, filling Mags with assurance that he approved of both message and medium. 'You're bleedin' beautiful. They're only massive, so they are.' He sounded deeply moved.

Mags thought his emotion a bit pathetic, and loved him all the more for that. Breathing shallow and fast, Dommo swallowed noisily. Between her legs his thigh moved slowly, and he kneaded her breasts with sweaty hands.

She closed her eyes, as delicious sensations emanated from her groin, and spread to every cell of her body.

Suddenly the massaging stopped, leaving her hanging from a precipice, as Dommo's head hit her collar bone with a painful bump. She waited impatiently for the stroking to resume, and when it didn't she opened her eyes.

'For fuck's sake, Dommo! You're not gonna goof-off on me now, are ya?' His head had dropped onto her breast, one ear nestled neatly in her cleavage. His open mouth dribbled ropes of curried saliva onto her naked flesh. 'Here, Dommo,' she said, shaking his wilting body, 'wake up, in the name a Jasus!'

'Goofin'? Who's goofin'-off?' he said, jerking into wakefulness. 'Come on, we'll have a gargle and hit the sack.' Trying to grab for the whiskey bottle, he knocked it over. Golden liquid poured onto the table and down to the lino before he got a grip of it, and put the bottle to his head. He drank deeply, then went to the ghetto-blaster, and after flinging Garry's tape across the room, put on one of his own.

Mags splashed vodka into a cup, and drank, oblivious to

the liquor trickling down betwen her naked breasts. The music sounded so good to her that she rushed over and turned up the volume.

Dommo danced around the room, bottle in hand. Whiskey gushed from the spout, as, jumping and waving his arms, he raved to the blaring synthsizer. Mags joined him in the manic dance.

The frantic din stopped between tracks, and the baby's screams became audible. Rushing over, Dommo grabbed her and held her above his head. As the new track gained a frantic beat, he matched it with the recklessness of his dancing, hopping from chair to chair and swinging the hysterical baby, who was turning blue in the face.

'Jasus, Dommo, stop that! Gis her to me!'

Dommo danced on, oblivious. The baby's mouth was wide open in a vain effort to breathe, shock choking her.

'Gimme me fuckin' baby.' Mags screamed so shrilly that she outdid the blaring music. Dommo stopped dead. His look stabbed through Mags' eyes, deep into her frightened brain. She went pale and cold with fear. Dommo was on a chair, holding the choking baby over his head.

Raising her arms, Mags pleaded silently.

'Here, ya can have your fuckin' little bastard,' he shouted, plonking the child roughly but safely into her arms. As the baby let out a reassuring howl, Dommo jumped off the chair, and smashed his fist onto the ghetto-blaster, silencing it before he sat heavily on the bed and started to undress.

Mags rocked Tracy until they were both somewhat calmer. She was terrified and deeply wounded by Dommo's words. That wasn't her Dommo! It musta been the whiskey what didn't agree with him, she thought. She would make things better. Putting the baby, still distressed, in the cot, she went to him. He was sitting slumped on the bed, one shoe and sock off, trouser and underpants around his ankles, his head lolling on his chest.

'Ay Dommo, don't go to sleep on me now, love,' she said, trying hard to sound cheerful. Placing her hand just above his pubic hair, she massaged his flesh gently. 'What about it, Dommo love?'

He made no response.

Sex was the last thing Mags wanted after what had happened but she felt that they should not go to sleep without making up, and a bit of a ride would help him forget that she had shouted at him like that.

'Fancy a bit, Dommo?' she whispered. She jumped with fright at the speed with which he awoke. In an instant he seemed alert again.

'I'll tell ya what I fuckin'well want! I wanna know whose little bastard that is.'

Mags' emotions were stretched to snapping point. Between the heroin cascading through her veins, more booze than she had ever drunk before, and the scene with Dommo, she could suppress it no longer. After all those years of silence, it gushed up and she had to admit to the soul-killing pain.

''Twas me first holy communion.' She spoke in a sort of trance, as if her brain had no control over her mouth.

'Ya first holy comm'fuckin'union?'

'Yea! I'll never forget it. Seven year old, an' all dolled up like a little princess I was. Me poor ma worked months a overtime ta get alla that gear. White, that's mostly what I remember about that day. Well, the first half of the day! I was dressed from head to toe in white. Jasus, I thought I was great, I did. Me dress was all frills puffed out around me knees, and I'd this beautiful hat with a white veil. I never felt happier in me whole life, a princess for a day. I was so excira, me stomach was in rag order. When I got the stuff, the communion like, it stuck to the top of me mouth. You're not allowed to chew, ya know, cos it's the body of Christ. It's not chewing gum. You're supposed to swally it but I couldn't. I was mortified. I thought I'd be punished be God for this terrible thing goin' wrong in me mouth.'

Mags was pale and shaking. Tears ran down her cheeks. She gulped breath without interrupting the rush of her speech.

'Maybe that was it. Maybe I was punished cos I did sometin' wrong with me first holy communion? The priest in his big white dress was rabbitin' on; I couldn't understand a word a what he was sayin' but. Inanyway, after the priest was finished, me Ma an' Da, well, me step-da, brought me to a pub, an bought me Coke an crisps. I was delighra so I was cos it was me first time in a pub. Before, if they went for a jar, I'd have to wait outside, but this time was great. People were comin' up an buyin be Coke an chocolate an' things, and givin me money. It was only then, with the Coke an all, that I swallied the holy communion. Me Ma didn't drink much, but me step-da was knocking them back. I could see me poor Ma get worried when he got stuck into the whiskey. She had to go to work for a couple of hours. She did cleaning in the offices near the flats. But she had arranged it so she would not be gone for long.'

Talking at an ever-increasing gallop, Mags gulped a lungful of air. 'Then ja know what I did? Jasus, didn't I only spill his fuckin' pint all over me lovely dress an' his trousers. I started to bawl, an' me Da went to hit me a box, but didn't me Ma catch his fist. I'll always remember her beggin him not ta hit me cos it was me holy communion. An' ya know what? Didn't his face change into a big smile, an instead a given me a dig, he gave me a hug, an' said he'd let me off this time. Then I bawled all the more with the relief, an' cos me dress was knackered. Inanyway, it was arranged that me Ma would go to work, an' me Da would bring me home an' sponge off the wet clothes, an' me Ma would be along then to go with us to me uncles' an aunts' places.

'So he took me home to the flat, an' me snivellin' an' all snots an' bubbles. I was so ashamed I was, the neighbours were all gawkin' at me. So he got narky again, and warned me to shut it, or else! So I'm tellin ya, I shut it, rapid.

'The minute we got into the flat, he took off his trousers and started to sponge them down. If I wasn't so frightened, I'd a laughed at the look a him, standin' there in his best clobber, with no trousers on his big hairy legs. Even though I was scared of him, I still loved him, he was me Da, well ya know, the nearest thing to a Da I'd ever known. An' sure he had to give me a box every now and then, or else I'd a gone wild altogether.

'He comes over an' drags me dress off over me head. The clips nearly ripped the face offa me, and I saw buttons fly all over the kip. Well, Jasus, I really bawled then, so I did, an' he lashed out with the back of his hand an' boxed me across the ear. I went flyin' across the room and landed on the bed. The pain was awful. He came over to the bed an' I was expectin' another few digs, but he just stood there. When he did speak, he was really nice. He started sayin' he was sorry, that he loved me, an' that he'd never wallop me again. "Here come on," he says, "we'll get into bed, and I'll give ya a special hug that will make ya feel better."

'I used to love gettin' into bed with me Ma before he moved in with us ... it was warm an' safe like. So when we got into bed, I expected the same. There was a terrible smell a booze, but I didn't mind that, I was warm and safe, an' the tears began to dry up.

'But the cryin' never stopped. Me Da was bein' really nice. "Come here now," he says, an' started rubbin' me back, going farther up and down each time. "Now wasn't that nice," says he. "Turn round, and I'll give your belly a little rub to make ya feel nice." I didn't want to, but I couldn't say no cos he was bein' so nice. I loved him for forgivin' me boldness all mornin'. He spun me onto me back. "Now don't be afraid," he says, and the minute he did, I was in terror. Sometin' about the way he said it. He sounded scared himself like, an' his breathin' was quare. I went into a ball in the bed, but he pushed me legs down and started to rub me belly. I was so scared that I felt sick, an' I told him. "Ya'll feel great after this," he says, an' shoved his hand down between me legs. I nearly died.'

Mags' body shook, her silent tears turning to noisy sobs, yet she kept up the manic pace of her story between quick intakes of breath.

'I started to scream, "I'm gonna be sick, Daddy, I'm gonna voma!" But he put his hand over my mouth, an' the next of all, he rolled over onto me, crushin' me, an' smothering me with his smell. I felt this stabbin' between me legs. He was jammin somethin' sharp up the tender place where I did me wee wees, an' I thought I was gonna die with the tearin' pain. He was rippin' me soft little privates. I wanted to die, cos what was happenin' to me. I felt raw and full of pain. I thought me guts were gonna fall out the wound he was rippin' open. I was sick, but his hand was over me mouth, an' I was drownin' in Coke an' chocolate voma.'

Mags buried her face in her hands. She rocked silently on the edge of the bed, taking long quivering breaths before she carried on talking, now slower and calmer.

'He rolled offa me, an' I spewed up gallons a Coke an' crisps an' chocolate. Me holy communion must a come up with the rest. The next I remember, he was cleaning me all over with a wet rag. He was fully dressed, an' he kept on sayin' how this was our big secret, an' how I'd be sent away to a home, an' never see me Ma ever again, if I ever tole anyone.

'When me Ma came home an' saw me so sick an' sorry for meself, she thought it was all cos a eatin' too much sweets. I wanted to throw me arms around her and never let her go. I was afraid but. We rushed out to see me aunts and uncles. There was a big brown stain on me dress, an' it was all crumpled. I was ashamed of meself in front of them all. Ashamed of the dirt of me dress. Mortified because of the pain between me legs, an' the dirty things I'd done. Ashamed of me life, an' scared that he would do it to me again. And he did, again, an' again, an' again, till I got pregnant an' ran away from home when I was sixteen.'

Dommo sat in silence, head hanging in a pose which Mags interpreted as embarrassment. She craved reassurance, a kind word, a hug, anything!

'You're the first one I ever tole,' she said, nudging him with her elbow.

Dommo fell back across the bed, froth at the corner of his mouth, breathing evenly.

'Jasus' sake, Dommo, ja hear a word I told ya? Wake up, Dommo, wake up!' she shouted, shaking him. 'Jasus, don't tell me ya never heard a bleedin' word I was saying?'

Her tears had stopped. All her life she had wanted to share her hurt with someone, but if Dommo hadn't heard, it was probably just as well. Somehow just saying it out loud made her feel a little better. She was glad she had admitted the depth of her pain.

She looked at Dommo lying across the bed naked from the waist down, and had to laugh. She stared at his shrivelled, little-boy's penis, and laughed even more. The very idea of sex seemed stupid, absolutely disgusting! Why she ever fancied him shoving his smelly little thing into her, she could not think.

The drug in her veins was coercing with a golden warmth and her eyelids felt a ton weight. She crawled onto the bed, and managed to pull a blanket over herself and Dommo.

So, Dear Reader, our leading character was abused as a child. The author has just rubbed our noses in the gory details in order, no doubt, to make the case that, having been so abused, she is then to be forgiven for all her subsequent crimes. We are back to the hoary old 'I can't help what I do, I'm not responsible for my actions' chestnut.

We hear this kind of nonsense in the courts with monotonous regularity. Rapists, for example, often maintain that they are to be excused their horrendous crimes on the basis of their having themselves been abused as children.

But let me ask a simple question. If being a victim in childhood makes a rapist out of the abused, why then do females, who constitute the vast majority of victims, not go on to become the rapists of men? No! The thesis simply does not stand up to the scrutiny. People commit crimes from their own free choice.

There is an issue regarding this part of the text, however, which any intelligent reader will have been aware of, but the author has deliberately glossed over. I refer, of course, to 'parenting'. Mags was at a disadvantage! She suffered from the fact that her mother was out at work and not available to protect her child. And, as we have seen at the start of the text, and will see again, she suffered from having a weak, over-indulgent mother. Since Mags was not sent to prison for her first offence, she must have been very young when she drifted towards crime. Why did her mother not chastise her severely then, and save the courts from having to administer punishment later?

But if the author is guilty of having glossed over these issues, my detractors, the Dublin 4 set and the feminist set, would applaud this. For them, you see, a smack amounts to child abuse! The experience of hundreds of generations of parents is as nothing alongside their new-fangled psychological theories.

Well, all right, I too can appeal to that dubious science. The findings that I refer to are of a much later, and more mature, study by psychologists into the causes of crime, than my critics seem to have access to. I quote part of the findings from memory, but quite accurately, I assure you.

Psychologists have for a long time studied criminals classified as psychopaths, or in the latest jargon, 'sociopaths'. These people are aggressive, impulsive and anti-social individuals who appear to have little or no concern for society's values. The problem lies in identifying the causes of sociopathy. Concern with increasing incidents of violent crime has led psychologists to consider whether the sociopath personality is accompanied by changes in physiology.

Let us look at a simple example.

To learn not to steal, a child must be taught that it is wrong to take the property of others without their permission. The socialisation usually occurs within the family, where the appropriate fear response is developed. Children learn to fear punishment if they steal, and that fear enables them to inhibit their thieving impulses. Anti-social children, however, do not learn adequate fear responses, and so are unable to anticipate negative reactions if they steal. The body deals with emotions through a system of nerves called the Autonomic Nervous System (ANS, for short). The ANS controls the fear response. If children have quick ANS responses, they will learn to react to temptation with fear, which will inhibit their desire to steal. Children who have slow ANS responses do not have this safeguard. Research studies have indicated that those who exhibit criminal behaviour do tend to have slower ANS responses. Or, in plain English: psychology is eventually coming around to say what parents have known for thousands of years: a good smack is essential to the development of a healthy and happy child. A smack in time saves crime!

While on the topic of working mothers, there is another influence which women's liberation has had that is dramatised in the text but which, again, has been glossed over. Women's new-found freedoms are being abused by the poor. Whereas before, if there was a drinking problem in the house, it affected only the father, and the children could always count on one sober parent to protect them from the worst effects of the alcoholic parent, nowadays both parents may spend all their time in the pub. This and the advent of the drug culture account for another factor, which is that the percentage of women in prison in Ireland is rising slowly but surely. These problems have a cumulative effect over the generations, as we shall see from the text.

Swimming up through a treacly fog of distress, Mags came to a painful consciousness of the baby's crying. Through fragmented impressions and patchy memories, she became aware that she had been out of the nick for nearly a month. A frantic month of shooting up, of drops and pickups, dark-alley business and back-lane meetings, of coke and ecstasy, of opiates and heroin, of rushes and speeding, of paradise and heaven. And now of the infernal horrors of hell! She felt toxic. Her head and every bone in her body ached as the sunlight through the grimy window clawed at her eyes. Under a pile of soiled blankets, and dressed in her filthy tracksuit, she was chilled to the core of her being. The baby's crying rent her brittle eardrums.

Focusing with difficulty, she saw Dommo sitting on the settee, shooting up.

'Gis that over when you're finished,' she croaked, dragging herself from under the blankets, and with shaking hands lifted the crying baby. Dommo was lost in the first rush of the drug and didn't answer. 'Here, gis it, will ya for Jasus' sake, quick! I'm strung out to fuck so I am!'

Dommo started to disassemble the syringe.

'I said, gis it over. Ya deaf or wha'?' Peeling the piss-soaked sleepysuit off Tracy, Mags scraped the disintegrated nappy into hot balls of cottony shit, exposing a mass of sores on red-raw flesh. The acidic smell scalded Mags' nostrils.

'Sorry about that, love,' Dommo said cheerily; 'there's none left.'

'Wha'?' she shouted, and glared, mad-eyed, into his broad smile.

'There's none left, so there's not.'

'Ya don't mean to say ya used it all?' Her voice shook, with only the possibility that he might be winding her up for a laugh keeping her from hysteria.

Still smiling, he took the baby, returned her to the cot and took Mags in his arms. She wanted to escape, but was trapped like the women in the Dracula video. Somehow she managed to break the spell of his all-seeing, shiny-plastic eyes and to get out of his grip. She picked up her child and managed to lull it to mere whimpering.

'Wha' happened to the bag a gear what Garry gave ya?' she asked wearily, keeping a prudent eye on his expression.

'Had to give some free samples,' he said, bringing his face closer to hers, 'ya wide, Mags love? To get the business goin'. An' I had to pay back a bit to a few guys for when I was inside. Ya know what I mean like?'

'Sure,' she stammered before breaking down in tears.

113

'Now we owe Garry two grand but.' Hysteria mounted in her as she continued, shouting between gasps for breath. 'An' we've nuttin' left ta use, nuttin' arall! What are we gonna do now, Dommo, what are we gonna do in the name a Jasus?'

'Ah snap out of it for fuck's sake! It's not the end of the bleedin' world, so its's not!'

'It's not the end of the fuckin' world for you,' Mags yelled, terrifying the baby. 'It's all fuckin' right for you, so it is. You can laugh cos ya bombed outa ya fuckin' bollix, so ya are. You can stand there with a stupa big grin on ya ugly mush an'–'

An unmerciful explosion erupted in her left ear and Mags crashed back, landing on the floor and smashing her head off the wall. Instinctively, she held the baby to her breast. The pain on the side of her head was excruciating, but she had no idea what had happened. There was a loud ringing noise and a brain-scorching confusion of electric sparks. She felt something grab her, and her head started to hit the wall.

As unconsciousness began mercifully to intervene, Dommo's shouts vied with the noise of her head pounding the wall.

'Listen to me ... cunt ... my fuckin' gaff ... no poxy ... tells me ... my bleedin 'gear ... scumbag ...'

Mags sunk into dark oblivion.

When she came to, she was stretched out on the bed. Straining the one eye that could see through the swelling, she focused on Dommo, who, head in hands, was sitting on the end of the bed crying. Mags groaned with pain and his head jerked up, relief transforming his wet and dirty face.

'Jasus, Mags! Ya all right, love? Thanks be ta Jasus an' his holy mother.' He went to the top of the bed and took her battered head in his arms. Blood seeped into his World Cup tee-shirt. 'Christ, I don't know what got into me, Mags, honest I don't. I'll never do antin like that again, love. I swear on me mother's grave, Mags.' He burst into tears again, big sobs jerking his shoulders. Despite her own excruciating pain, Mags' heart went out to him. She squeezed his hand as tears flowed down her cheeks. Above the high-pitched siren in her ear, she became aware of the baby's crying.

'Tracy. Jasus, me poor baby!' She tried to lift herself out of Dommo's arms, but the pain in her head froze her. Dommo stood and put her head gently back on the blood-soaked pillow.

'Stay there love. I'll look after Tracy.'

The large circle of blood on his tee-shirt frightened her. Gingerly she brought her hand up the back of her head and taking it away, looked in horror at her finger's sticky redness.

She watched him strip and clean the baby. Expertly, he washed and creamed Tracy's flaming red bottom, which now had several open sores. Having changed her into a new nappy and a not too dirty sleepy-suit, he rocked her as he prepared a bottle. Sprinkling a few drops of warm milk on the back of his hand, he gave the teat to the child. Silence fell, as she sucked urgently, satisfying her ten-hour hunger. The sucking sounds came from further and further away and faded out altogether as Mags again lost consciousness.

A brutally clear memory of what had happened snapped into place as she came to for the second time. The pain had eased, but her head throbbed and the side of her face was aching from the beating. All the other hurts she recognised as withdrawals. Her back was sore and pains ran down her legs. She was chilled to the bone and her nose was running thick mucus. She knew the stomach cramps to be the onset of diarrhoea. Every pore craved heroin.

The baby was sleeping in her cot and Dommo was sprawled in an armchair, head thrown back, mouth open, saliva shining on his chin. His eyelids showed slits of bloodshot white. The lucky bastard, Mags thought. She tried to move on the bed to ease the pain and he woke. He went to her sheepishly.

'You're awake, Mags. I was outa me head with worry about ya, so I was.'

She looked into his gaunt face. He had lost a lot of weight since getting out of prison. So had she with all the running around, and living on chocolate and lemonade. The drugs had robbed them of their appetites, leaving a craving for sweet things to keep their blood sugar levels high enough and power the quest to satisfy their obsession.

Dommo's eyes were almost focused now. He seemed to be genuinely repentant, but what melted her heart was his look of fear.

He sat on the bed looking down at her like a child begging forgiveness. 'I don't know what got into me fuckin' head, Mags.' Tears flowed down his face. 'I'm outa me head with bleedin' worry, so I am. I need you, Mags, I need you.'

She needed to be needed by him. And sure everyone got a few digs from their fella every now and then; it was only natural, she thought. How else would ya know that they loved ya? Inanyway, she deserved it, getting stroppy with him like that.

It wasn't the punches that hurt, it was the withdrawals, and Dommo would sort that out for her somehow, she knew. She opened her arms and Dommo fell lightly down onto her. They wept pathetically.

'What are we gonna do, Dommo?'

'I'll think a sometin', don't worry, love.'

She took her head off his shoulder. 'I thought ya had a plan!'

'I have, Mags, I swear. But I can't put it into action till the cops get off me back. They're watchin' me like a hawk, the fuckers. I can't even deal the way they're houndin' me.'

She gently pushed Dommo off her and dragged herself up to make a cup of tea to wash down some painkillers.

'Where's the tablets were here the other day?'

'I used the last a them yesterday, Mags.'

'The teabags?'

'There somewhere.'

'Sure!' she said, flinging the empty box towards the rubbish bag. She went back to bed and put her bloodied head in her hands. 'I need a fix, Dommo! I need a bleedin' fix an' I need it fast! Ya'll have to go to Garry. Tell him ya'll pay

116

him after ya do the big job ya've planned.'

'For fuck's sake, I can't! I owe him two bleedin' grand, remember?'

'Just ask him for enough for a fix,' she pleaded, 'for the two of us, Dommo.'

'I can't fuckin' well go to Garry,' he screamed, sticking his nose to within an inch of her anguished face. 'Ya deaf or wha'?'

Mags tensed up again with the shock of his outburst. She sat on the bed as if she had a time-bomb on her lap.

Taking her rigid body in his arms, he rocked her.

'It'll be all ri', Mags, trust me,' he said but she could feel him shaking. He was in the early stages of withdrawal himself now, she could tell.

'I have it all sussed,' he said. 'This is what we do, ri'? We get a few quid, ya wide? Even 60 or 80 will do, and we'll buy enough gear to get us straigh'. Not from Garry but. We'll go easy on it, only use a bit like, and we'll sell the rest. I know where there's loads a yuppies who'll pay twice the price what I can get it for. Ya wide? The fuckin' yuppies are only weekend junkies; they don't have a clue. We can cut it ta fuck an' make a good bit on it. Put in a bit of flour or talc. Antin' white; they're too stupa to know the differ. Then I'll start to pay Garry back an' we're in business.'

'Sounds great but where will we get the first bit of money?'

'What time is it? Nine o'clock, Friday night, perfect. Ri', get dressed in ya best clobber. We're goin' for a pint.'

'It's not a bleedin' jar I want.'

'This is business Mags. I'll get a couple a handbags no bother.'

'What about the cops? I thought they were on ya back!'

'They are, but I'll be all ri' for a couple a snatches once you're with me. I'm just out for a jar with me bird, like anybody else on a Friday night.'

'What about Tracy? I can't leave her.'

'Look, we'll only be half an hour. I can't go alone, Mags, I'd stick out like a spare prick at a wake.'

117

'Jasus, I don't know, Dommo?'

'Don't know me bollix! Look, ja want a fix or don't ya? I only fed her an hour ago when ya were ... er, sleepin'. She'll be game ball.'

'Ya sure we won't get caught, Dommo?'

'Trust me, Mags. Trust me.'

Her aching body and throbbing head gave her no alternative but to trust to Dommo's skills. Forgetting the baby, she rushed to the sink, washed the congealed blood from the back of her head, and with shaking hands smeared make-up over her bruised face. Eyeshadow and lipstick streaked over larger areas than she wanted, but she made do.

Dommo put on his suit. It had been the height of fashion before he had gone into prison the last time. Now, Mags thought, he looked like something out of a Beatles movie; it was far too big for his gaunt frame. His runners looked stupid with the suit, and he needed a shave.

They went up a hill and came to a large church.

'Is that where they made the fillim about the hunchback what fell in love with the young one?'

'Yea, Christ Church. Jasus, were ya never on the south side before?'

'Was! Often. Just never saw that kip, that's all.'

'There's a big rugby match on tomorrow, all the Prod doctors will be kickin' the shit outa one another in Lansdowne Road. Grafton Street should be packed.'

Dommo was back in business. The quest was on, and he felt that old buzz he loved so much. Out on the streets planning a snatch, he was a man battling for survival. The warrior male was hunting, stalking his quarry. Something primeval in him made his heart beat faster. He felt sorry for the ordinary punters who got their meagre wages in boring jobs, or shuffling along in the dole queue, hand out pleading for a pittance. This was the life for him, a life of skill and bravery, devoid of hypocrisy.

They hurried down Dame Street and turned right towards Grafton Street. Jogging to keep up with Dommo,

Mags could not believe the change in him. He was excited, yet cool and professional.

'Ri', just goin' for a pint. But we don't have the price of a fuckin' pint, so just do as I tell ya.'

They were stopped from entering the first bar that Dommo chose by a pair of dress-suited doormen.

'Sorry sir, we're full.'

Dommo turned and walked away. 'Fuckin' scumbags! I'd a decked the two a them only we can't afford trouble now.'

He rejected several bars in the Grafton Street area. At one he knew the bouncer on the door, a long termer recently released from the Joy. They exchanged the slightest of knowing grins. The patch was off bounds.

It was getting near closing time and they were in a pub in Baggot Street before he saw his opportunity. Mags noticed heads turn and stare as they entered. She felt shabbily dressed among these immaculately turned out yuppies, and wished she had covered her black eye with make-up better before coming out. Dommo pointed to a long seat in the crowded bar and Mags sat down. He took off his jacket and he put it on the seat near her.

'Keep me place an' I'll get a jar. Wha' ja fancy – the usual?' he said over his shoulder, striding up to the busy counter, where he stood for a moment. He went back to Mags. 'Come on love, we'll go next door, it's too busy here, can't get served.'

Taking up his jacket, he sauntered out followed by Mags. Once out, they walked briskly along the road and turned down by the canal. Dommo looked over his shoulder, and skipping over a low wall, went to the tree-darkened stretch beside the water. Mags scrambled after him. Taking his jacket off his arm, he exposed a leather handbag.

'Jasus! Where ja get that?'

Dommo put on his jacket, and sitting on the grassy bank of the canal, emptied the bag's contents into his lap. Tissues and envelopes, an address book and make-up, tumbled out. He examined each item carefully before throwing them into the water. Mags wanted to ask for the cosmetics, but his temper was rising, so she didn't dare speak as he threw them into the canal with rising venom. He held up a single condom between the tips of his fingers as if it was infectious.

'Would ya lukka! The filthy yuppie cunt! Jasus, you'd think butter wouldn't melt in their bleedin' mouths, an' under it all they're goin' round like bitches in heat, bullin' for a fuck!' He threw the condom into the water and continued his search, pocketing credit cards and the coins. Viciously, he started pulling the bag asunder. Finding nothing more, he flung the tattered leather into the water. 'Fuck it, the dirty bitch musta had her money in a pocket. Bollix to it inanyway, and it's closin' fuckin' time. Too late to get in anywhere. Now we're really fuckin' snookered.'

Mags felt the wet grass soak into her clothes but it was the least of her discomforts. She was misery itself. The withdrawals were intolerable.

'If I even had a couple a score, I could get a bit a gear,' Dommo said pathetically. 'I mean sixty pound an' we're made! Ya know what I mean?'

'I know, I know, but what can I do?'

'Me last bird was great like that all the same ... always able to turn a couple a score in an emergency.'

'What ya tellin' me that for? I thought ya hated her?'

'I do, the poxy bitch. It's you I'm mad about, Mags, ya know that.' He put an arm around her shoulder and pulled her to him. 'Ya know I would do antin for you, Mags,' he said in a curious tone. 'Ya were never stuck for the price of a fix with her around but.'

Mags had noticed the activity on the road running beside the canal, with women being picked up and let off by men in cars. At some deep level of her confused consciousness she had understood, but had never dreamt that it could be any of her business. Incredulous, she broke free of Dommo's hypnotic stare. 'Dommo, are you sayin' ...' she trembled, 'are you suggestin' ...'

'T'would only be for a while, couple a weeks at the most,

till the pigs get offa me back an' I can get a chance to do this job. Honest, I swear, we'll be rollin' in it, our own BMW, holliers in the Costa what's it, the lot!'

Suddenly Mags jumped to her feet. 'Jasus, the baby! We've been out for ages.'

'Look,' Dommo shouted, jumping up and grabbing her in a painful grip, 'this is the story, ri'? Ya can fuck off home now an' leave me to try for a snatch. What with all the cops around here at this time a night gives me fuck all chance of gettin' away, an' you can go cold turkey in the flat alone. Or, ya can turn a couple a tricks an' be home within the hour, warm and snug with enough stuff for us and a bit to sell. What's it to be?' He released his grip but he continued to stare at her. She looked away, fearing his gaze.

She could see the poorly lit road. A car pulled up, a woman talked at the open window for a moment, got in and the car drove away. Just looking at the scene terrified Mags. But the horrors of withdrawal terrified her more! When she spoke, it was in a shaky whisper. 'What will I do? What do I say? What will they want?'

'Just walk up to where ya woman was, ri'? When one stops, just tell him it's twenty quid for a hand job, forty for the business. Nobody kisses ya,' he said, his face darkening. 'Ri'? It's just business, he pays the money and ya do the business, there's no kissin' or cuddlin' or any a that shit! Business only. They can't buy my bird, so they can't.'

Mags was sobbing hard now. She tried to ask a question but couldn't.

'Just get him to drive through the traffic lights; there's a real dark bit there. An' get him to bring ya back here after. Get the money first but! Ri'? Ya'll be OK, so ya will. If anyone gives ya any fuckin shit, scrawb the face offa him an roar. I'll be waitin' here, an if ya have any trouble, I'll have it sorted out rapid.'

Dragging herself up onto the road like an old woman with arthritis, Mags took her place on the pavement and whispered urgently down into the darkness. 'Ya sure ya know where we can get some gear at this time a night?'

'I'm sure, I'm sure. Trust me. Walk up an down a bit, slowly like, so's the cops can't do nuttin'.'

Mags walked unsteadily, expecting her legs to buckle under her at any moment. A rusty muck-splattered Ford Cortina squeaked to a stop beside her.

So much for the rich fuckers in their Mercs, she thought, just my luck. She was ready to run if the guy looked dangerous. He did not. In fact, she thought, he looked pathetic. He was old, fifty at least, she guessed, his face wrinkled and sunburnt. A culchie, with peaked cap askew exposing a milky white baldness, badly camouflaged by a few long grey hairs glued across the top of his head.

'Good night, missie,' he whispered, checking up and down. 'Is it doing business you are?' His voice shook like a little boy about to cry.

She would have loved to break down herself, then maybe he would pity her and give her the price of a fix. She swallowed hard. 'Twenty pound for a hand job,' she snapped.

'Oh, I see missie, and what about, er, what do you charge now for 'em ...'

'Forty pound for the business.'

'I will, er, take that so, missie.'

Jasus Christ! She thought, he wants his hole! How could she do that with the dirty old bastard? Dommo and herself had never got around to having sex, not that she could remember anyway! And before, it had only ever been done to her by that scumbag, her step-da! God, it would be the same all over again. How could she bring herself to do it with this stranger?

She wanted to run. She wanted to vomit. But most of all she wanted a fix! And if she could survive being done by an awl fella when she was just a little girl, she could survive it now! She would do it this once! It would be over in a minute, then never again!

'Missie? Missie?' His pathetic voice penetrated her brain. 'I'll give you the forty pounds so.'

'No, I was just thinkin', I'm too busy tonight. It will cost ya sixty pound.'

'Oh! Yes, well all right, but that's all the money I have on me,' he said, as if about to break down in tears. 'Will you get into the car?'

Mags got in. Now that she was committed, she began to feel business-like enough to get her through it without dying of shame and disgust.

'Where will I drive, missie?'

Jasus, what a stupid scumbag he was, with his 'missie' this and 'missie' that.

'Through those lights, and stop under the trees.'

The smell of the farmyard wafted from his body, and his big grimy hands shook on the wheel, as he drove the couple of hundred yards. His pot belly stretched the polyester stitches in his jumper to bursting point. A luminous statue of the Virgin Mary vied with a depressed and bloody-handed Padre Pio for the most prominent position on the dashboard.

The car jerked to a squeaky stop in the darkness, and the driver continued to stare out the front windscreen, hands clamped on the wheel as if he was still driving. The silence was broken only by his noisy swallowing. His breathing was strange and filled the car with its foul odour, adding to Mags' nausea.

For Jasus' sake, she thought, is he just going to sit there? Does he think I'm gonna seduce him, or what?

Mags could still get out of it, she thought. She could ask for the money, and when she had got it, leg it out of the car. He might, however, suspect something if she asked and drive away in panic. Better not to chance anything on the silly little fucker, with his three long hairs stretched over his baldy head.

'Well, ja want it or don't ya?' she asked.

'I do missie, I do.' The quiver in his voice was even worse now. He was still holding the steering wheel, and Mags could see his white knuckles. He continued to stare straight ahead.

Christ, she hated him. She loathed his ugliness, his stupidity, his foul smell. If she got through this ordeal, she would never do it again.

'Here, for fuck's sake,' she said, and squeezing her eyes shut, took his hand off the wheel and put it up her jumper and onto her breast. His hot sticky hand stayed limp. She opened her eyes, about to tell him to get on with it, or pay up and fuck off, but his appearance stopped her.

He was a mirror image of her own suffering. Eyes screwed closed, tears ran down his ruddy cheeks. Like a new born baby, he was all wrinkled fear and pain, and she was moved to pity. She had to stop herself from weeping for this elderly virgin, and all the suffering of the world. Christ, she wished she had never been born!

'Ah here, I'm not all that bad, for Jasus' sake,' she chided, somehow managing to sound cheerful, as, lifting her jumper up, she pulled his head down onto her naked breast. 'Now, isn't that nice?' She could feel his tears running down her belly, as a passing car swept a glaring beam over them. In the brief light she saw a man dressed in green on a bench near them. He had his back to them now, but she was sure he was getting his rocks off by spying on them. She was beyond caring, and hoped he enjoyed what he was seeing, the big green fool. She put her hand onto the sobbing man's lap and, with great difficulty, undid his trouser button, causing his zip to burst open and release an avalanche of blubber onto his lap. Groping under the distended belly, she found the lifeless blob of flesh, and massaged it. She lifted herself off the seat, and pulled her tights and knickers down around her ankles in one quick movement. Dragging his damp and smelly body over onto her, she tried to guide the flaccid little thing into her.

It was no good: she was dry and closed; he was limp. Beyond revulsion, she managed to ignore the smell and sweat, wanting to be responsible for him having a second or two of pleasure. Maybe that would be the best thing she would do for the rest of her life: give a lonely old man his hole.

She was still willing to try, but a change in the rate of his sobbing, and warm sticky wetness, turning to cold between

124

her thighs, announced her partial failure.

He was still and quiet for a few seconds and then rolled off her. Fishing about frantically under his car seat, as Mags wiped between her legs and rearranged her clothes, he threw a brown envelope into her lap, a wad of notes fanning out of it. Without him closing his trousers, he had the engine running, was releasing the clutch, and the car was moving away. She opened the door and jumped out.

'Don't fucking mention it,' she shouted after the speeding car.

A hand landed on her shoulder and she screamed. It was Dommo.

'Jasus, ya frightened the livin' shit outa me.'

'I was comin' ta get ya. Ya could a had a dozen tricks in that time. Ja have trouble with the fucker, or wha'?'

'Nuttin' I couldn't handle.'

'He better have paid ya for all that time,' he said, whipping the envelope from Mags' hand. She nodded in the direction of the guy on the bench and they scurried up the canal towards Rathmines. Dommo counted as they walked. The banknotes were so crisp and clean, they might have been washed and ironed.

'Fair play ta ya, Mags, a hundred notes. He musta enjoyed hisself.' He stopped walking. 'Ya didn't let him kiss ya, did ya?'

'Course not, dirty awl fucker.'

'I have a contact up here in Rathmines, fuckin' yuppie, he sells good gear but. It'll only take a couple of minutes to get there.'

'Thanks be ta Jasus.'

'Ja want to go straight back to the kid? She might be awake be now. I'll get the gear and bring it back to ya.'

Mags' brow furrowed. 'Ah she'll be all right for another little while.'

The obscene conduct described above, Dear Reader, was what my critics would have us believe was a victimless crime, and therefore a facet of human activity in which the forces of law and order should have no function! I will resist the tempta-tion to return to this topic and point out further absurdities in that theory, since I know that you will do that for yourself. Perhaps, however, I should explain where they derive that silly notion from.

We shall look at the concept and development of law later, but suffice it to say here that not everyone agrees on how and why laws came about at all. Two major models have developed to explain this process: 'concensus' and 'conflict' models.

The concensus' approach sees law as the formalisation of the views and values of the people. It sees law as having evolved from social interaction, reflecting the values of society, and eventually becoming formalised. Underlying the laws is a concensus of values held by the people.

The contrasting position is the conflict approach which postulates that conflict among various groups in society is resolved when the groups in power achieve control. The law, therefore, serves the interests of the party in power. It follows from this appoach that laws which attempt to regulate sexual behaviour are passed because the party in power wishes to enforce its morality on others, even when the practises against which they legislate are engaged in by themselves. The law becomes a symbol of middle-class power.

It appears obvious to me that the concensus approach is by far the more accurate explanation of the development of laws. It goes without saying, however, that the approach to which my critics subscribe is the conflict approach! 'Conflict in all things' must be their motto! By way of criticism of this approach, let me simply point out that among the motley crew with whom they share this view are the (last few) followers of Karl Marx.

Acceptance of the conflict approach not only leads to absurd ideas like that of the 'victimless crime', but to even more dangerous notions like the labelling theory. If you will allow me to digress somewhat to explain this theory, I think you will be amused, as well as alerted, to the depths of stupidity to which criminology can descend when in the hands of radicals.

Most theories ask why the individual committed the crime, and what can be done to prevent such actions in the future. They look for answers in the individual physique, hormones, in the environment, or in social processes, but always asking why the person engaged in the behaviour. Labelling theorists, in contrast, ask why the person was designated as deviant. For them, the issue is not the behaviour, but why the behaviour was labelled deviant. They are not interested in what was done, but in how people react to what was done. They hold that only some people who engage in certain types of behaviour are labelled deviant, while some are not, and it is the reason of this distinction which interests them.

Some men drink too much and are called alcoholics, while others who drink too much are not. Some people behave oddly and are committed to mental hospitals, while others who behave oddly continue to live peaceably in society. The differences are determined by how the community responds to and codes the behaviour which comes to its attention.

If criminal behaviour is therefore to be explained according to the responses of others, rather than the characteristics of the offender, the appropriate subject matter for study will be the audience, not the criminal. Only the reaction of others will determine whether or not the behaviour will be labelled deviant.

For the person labelled 'deviant' because of some initial minor criminal action, secondary deviation will, the theorists insist, be a necessary social role which becomes a means of defence or adaptation to the problems created by the societal reaction to the primary deviation. A criminal is made, they say, by society describing, defining, segregating, making the criminal self-concious, and so evoking the very traits that are

127

complained of.

The people who are most likely to be labelled deviant are those on the margins of society, and once they are labelled, they usually cannot escape the designation. The theory holds that it does not matter whether the valuation is made by those who would punish or by those who would reform. The person becomes the thing he is described as being. The very enthusiasm of the labellers defeats their aim. The harder they try to reform evil, the greater the evil grows under their influence.

The fault, Dear Reader, we are told by these ingenious criminologists, lies with the labellers ... that is, with the law-abiding citizens. It is these citizens who create deviance by making rules which, when broken, constitute crime, and by applying those rules, label innocents as guilty.

Once a person is labelled deviant, he is given a new identity, and through degrading ceremonies, he becomes, in the eyes of those who condemn him, a different person.

Once labelled, the new criminal has an impossible task to shed that status. The effects of labelling may also snowball in that once a person is stigmatised by the label, new restrictions are placed on legitimate opportunities and the probability of further deviance is increased.

Their wonderful, indeed magical, solution is simply not to call evil behaviour evil. The less said the better, these theorists hold. And quite frankly, the less said about the labelling theory, conflict theories, victimless crime, and other such drivel, the better!

So back to the text, and to more 'harmless' victimless crime, which is considered crime at all only because it has been so labelled by intolerant, law-abiding citizens with no appreciation for cultural diversity!

Scurrying up the bank of the Grand Canal as quickly as her heels would allow, Mags was alone in the dark except for an occasional kerb crawler. She was finished for the night. The drug was wearing off fast, and within a few minutes she would be having withdrawals, and would be aware of what she did in the cars, of the horror of her reality. For now, heroin cushioned her in a celebration of unawareness. She could never face the nightly ordeal 'straight' again.

The supplier to whom Dommo had introduced her on that first night she had worked the canal did not deal after one o'clock in the morning. 'Draws too much attention,' he said. Her last customer had been yet another hornless wonder. She should have known because he had cruised around, slowing down beside her and speeding away again, before he got the bottle to stop for business. A sure sign he wanted the mammying treatment before he could get it up. Now she was dashing to reach the dealer in time.

As she turned into Rathmines Road, running to beat the hands on the Tower clock, she thought of how she was always in a hurry: leaping out of the bed as soon as Tracy started to bawl; frantically getting a fix ready; dashing around looking after the kid until she went to sleep, then flying out with Dommo to try to snatch a bag; scurrying about grabbing and fighting, arguing and threatening; dashing back to the flat, feeding the kid, shooting up and starting the whole frenzied procedure all over again before rushing down the canal to do the night shift. Life was frantic – never a moment to relax, never an instant to think. The weight was falling off her.

Occasionally, she enjoyed some time with Tracy. There was nothing like a turn-on to help you enjoy playing baby games. But of late the turn-ons were only bringing her back to some feeling of normality, the beautiful rushes and orgasmic thrills were less frequent, even though she was using ever-increasing amounts of the narcotic. Playing with the kid was becoming a drag.

Mags got to the house in Rathmines a bit after one o'clock, but the deal was done and she caught a taxi back to the flat through the grey drizzle. As the taxi turned a corner into Dame Street, the headlights lit up an old tramp shuffling across the road. The driver stopped in good time, but the lights shone for a second on the tramp's terrified face. Since Mags was in her early stages of withdrawal, the old man's fear reminded her of her day-time activities.

All the bars within walking distance were copping on to herself and Dommo. Usually they got lucky with a snatch once or twice a day, but they were always small hauls, thirty or forty notes, carefully folded in pension books, not enough to keep them high for the morning. The tramp's face reminded her of her first snatch, an ancient old woman shuffling home from the post office with her pension in her bag clamped under her arm. She had tried to hold on to the bag, and in the tussle had fallen. Mags had trod on her hand and felt the bones crackle. The look of terror in the pathetic old eyes and the pleading whimpers she made in her brittle-brave effort to hold on to her miserable couple of pounds had haunted Mags for days.

But for days only! After that there was a period when everything had conspired against them, and she had gone through cold turkey for the first time.

The hell she went through paid for all her wrong-doings and justified any effort to get straightened out again. She was made holy by the pain of withdrawal. In a tightly sealed system of drug-induced morality, she worked for her highs and paid for them a million times over by the lows. Cocooned in a vile skin of self-justifying and self-perpetuating actions, she was on a roller-coaster of need. Plunging down into the troughs of despair demanded heroin to get her up the other side. Once up, there was nowhere to go but down again. Anyone who suffers like a junkie is liberated from the ties of normal morality. The junkie suffers to such an extent that only the bliss of heroin can make amends for the pain.

Jumping out of the taxi, Mags threw the driver a tenner and headed up the stairs to the flat. She was later than usual and obsessed with latching on to the nourishing nipple of the needle.

Dommo, pale and edgy, was pacing the floor.

'What the fuck kept ya?'

'Nuttin'! Why?' she said with the assurance of the breadwinner. But she wasn't forgetting the beating he had once given her and so walked a fine line between standing up for herself and pushing him too far.

'Ja get the gear?'

'Course! How's Tracy?'

'Game ball, snorin' the head offa herself.'

'Ah, you're great, love.' She threw him the package. He cooked a generous quantity of the gear and, unable to get a vein anywhere, injected into the artery between his legs. If business was slow and Mags got home very late, he would be in such a state that he could not manage to get his own fix ready. She hated when that happened because then she had to get it ready and inject it for him. It nearly made her sick to see all the scabs around his testicles and on his penis, where he used to inject until the vein collapsed.

In the two months since she had started working the canal, she had been raking in more and more money each night as she learned the tricks of the trade. There was no more spending half an hour with the one customer. She had it down to a few minutes.

By the end of the second week she had lost all fear. The customers were as quiet as mice, shivering and shaking as if they were about to have punishment, not sex.

Business was great. She was younger than most of the others and often saw cars slow down for one of them, then speed up and stop at her. Her skinny waist and big boobs were her greatest assets. She couldn't believe the amount of money they brought her in. Neither could she believe the amount of money they were pumping into her and Dommo's veins! There were nights when she earned four or five hundred pounds, all of which went on drugs. Dommo repaid the original bill to Garry in the first weeks, but now they were purchasing from several sources and using every pennysworth they could buy. It was not as if the drug was doing anything for her; it was just keeping her functioning, and even to achieve that required more each hit.

Taking the syringe from Dommo, she cooked up her own fix. Considering the amount of money she was making and that she felt so poorly, she thought she deserved a treat. Dommo was putting on a video. She cooked up twice as much as she had ever taken in one fix, about two hundred pounds' worth, found a good vein in her leg and injected.

Jesus Christ, she felt better! In fact she felt brilliant! That's what had been wrong. She had been too mean with herself, not treating herself to enough to get a good hit. Well now that she was earning big bucks, she wouldn't skimp any more. It was smashing that she was able to keep them in supplies with just a few hours of work each night. And when the cops got off Dommo's back, he would do the big job, they would settle down in a nice place and give up drugs. Jesus, life was great all the same!

While she hid the works, Dommo was laughing out loud at the video as he watched a man tearing the clothes from a pre-pubescent girl. The camera zoomed in on her budding breasts as he ripped her chest open and pints of blood spurted everywhere.

'Ah for fuck's sake, Dommo, I seen that one before!'

At last, Dear Reader, I find something in the text with which I can agree. I presume that the author intended to bring our attention to the horror of the gratuitous violence to which we are nowadays exposed on television and in videos. Forgive me if I digress to relate to you the latest findings from America on violence and the media.

There, research has shown that children spend more time watching television than on any other activity. By the time they are eighteen, the average child will have spent far more time in front of a television set than in the classroom. Adults spend about forty percent of their leisure time watching television, which means that television-viewing ranks third behind sleep and work as the occupier of adults' time.

The research has shown that television is the most

influential of the media for adolescents and has four types of effect on their social behaviour: the teaching of aggressive styles of conduct; the lessening of restraints on aggression; desensitisation and habituation to violence; and the shaping of images of reality on which people base their actions.

By the age of eighteen, the average person has witnessed over eighteen thousand murders on television. Sixty percent of prime-time television programmes contain violent solutions to conflicts, and cartoons are among the most violent. The data clearly suggest that a relationship exists between television and 'real world' violence. Depictions of violence on television teaches people that it is an acceptable means to an end. Children who watch violence on television are much less likely than those who do not, to stop other children from hurting one another. This desensitising effect has long-term anti-social consequences, extending as far as tolerance for war and other types of cultural violence.

Similar research has shown a casual relationship between exposure to pornography and aggressive behaviour towards women. I will not insult your intelligence, by dragging you through the research findings, when I know that you will accept this as a foregone conclusion.

But what exactly did our author think she was doing with her opus if not adding to the mass of pornography in the world? What kind of self-delusion was she suffering from when she implicitly criticised video violence in a text which is itself replete with graphic scenes of violence and sexual perversity?

Now, four months after her release, Mags' merry-go-round was getting more frantic every day. She grabbed a burger and chips most days, but she never sat down to a proper meal, and was reduced to a sickly six stone from her former nine. Chocolates and fizzy drinks were rotting her teeth fast; two from the front were missing and the rest were a technicolour fuzz. Her complexion was a pale green, punctuated by

133

blotches and pimples. Her hair was lank and thinning. Her breasts sagged, and her nose was flattened, creased and purple. Except in the earliest rush of a turn-on, she was depressed and nervous. She carried a knife hidden in her clothes when working and hated every customer with a vengeance.

This rapid physical and emotional degeneration, the fear and the black hatred, were all very much connected.

One night, a guy who had been slowing down at the various women and then driving on, stopped for Mags. Her youthful good looks had been fading but, back then, were still very marketable. She had taken a good turn-on before coming out and felt fine. Knowing that this bloke had been kerb-crawling for an hour, she was not very interested, but on the other hand, the car was a big expensive-looking job, so she decided to give him a try.

She knew she had made a mistake the second she sat into the car, but there was nothing for it then except to brazen it out and try and keep the upper hand. About thirty years of age, he was big and strong, his blond hair cut very short. His features were perfect, yet Mags found him revolting to look at.

'Just drive through the lights and stop under the trees,' Mags said.

'You're joking me, woman.' The accent was Dublin 4. 'Anybody could see us there! I know a lane that would do much better,' he said, speeding past her usual spot.

'Ri', ya have ta leave me back to here but.'

He made no reply.

'Ja hear what I'm sayin' to ya? Me fella follies me if I'm missin' long.'

The bluff didn't seem to register.

'He takes all a me customers' reg numbers, so he does.'

He looked at her, grinning. 'Is that so?'

As he drove down a long dark lane off Fitzwilliam Street which she knew to be a dead end, she checked the door discreetly but found that it was centrally locked. At the end of

134

the empty lane, he stopped the car and switched off the lights, leaving a green glow from the instrument panel. He turned in his seat and stared at her.

'Do you enjoy the practice of your profession?'

'Wha'?'

'Your work ... do you enjoy it?'

'It's work.'

'Yes, but what aspects of it do you enjoy most?'

'Wha'?'

'What bits of your job do you enjoy best? Do you enjoy being fucked by half-a-dozen different men each night? Do you have an orgasm with them all or just some of them?'

'A wha'?'

'Do you come with all your customers?'

Her brain was speeding. Knowing that he was not fooled by her tough act, she changed tack.

'I'd come with *you*,' she said, massaging the back of his bull neck, 'so I would, big boy.'

'You better!'

'Let's do it then, ya sexy hunk ya.' She brought her hand slowly down his stomach and, after rubbing his groin, started to open his zip. Much to her relief, he had an erection. 'Jasus, it's huge so it is,' she forced herself to say.

Pressing a button on the side of her seat, making it fall into a reclining position, he proceeded to pull at her clothes.

'Go easy, big boy! Wait till I get ya all ready.' She took his trousers and underpants down, a difficult procedure she usually did not bother with, and started to massage his swollen gland.

'Get your clothes off,' he barked.

She rolled her mini skirt up around her waist, exposing her nakedness ... she had long since given up wearing knickers.

'Get your damn clothes off,' he said, squinting his eyes.

She stripped off her meagre items of clothing as quickly as she could, hoping that he did not sense her panic. Her shaking hand returned to its task.

'Suck it.'

'I don't ...'

Grabbing her by the hair he forced her face into his lap. In spite of having in the past been offered huge money, she would never give oral sex. Now she struggled to avoid vomiting over his foul-smelling gland as, with a painful knot of her hair in his fist, he jerked her head up and down. She tried to make him come as quickly as possible to get the ordeal over, but there was no sign that he might. She attempted to raise her head to plead with him, but he held her in a vice-like grip.

He flung her back into the reclining seat, hitting her head off the door. 'You couldn't give a decent blow job if it was to save your life, you stupid cunt.' Rolling over onto her, he forced himself into her arid body. Despite the pain of his brutality, she felt some relief. Being dead from the waist down, she did not really care that he was plunging viciously in and out of her. Latching on to both of her breasts, he squeezed until she thought she would burst. She fought her need to scream in pain, and managed to speak into his ear. 'God, oh God! That's so good. I love it, I love it.'

She had never pretended to come before. She had never come with a man before. Her life might depend on her acting this time though. Sweating and grunting, he was burning the tender tissue of her vagina. With every agonising thrust of his body, she could feel a blister form inside her.

'Come into me, come into me,' she begged. 'I love it, I love it,' she lied through her tears.

He started to go soft inside her and his plunging stopped. He stayed motionless on her bruised and burning body. The knowledge that he had not been satisfied heightened her fear and she lay under his body like a rabbit in the jaws of a fox.

'Is there sometin' wrong, love?' she whispered, praying it was the right thing to say.

Letting go of her mangled breasts, he lifted himself up on his arms and stared down into her eyes. The colour had drained from his face.

'Don't "love" me, you whore,' he spat in a hissing whisper. 'And yes, as a matter of fact, there is something wrong.' His voice was rising. 'There is something very fucking wrong. You!' he yelled down into her face. 'You're what's wrong, you filthy cunt. You smell like a sewer,' he screamed. 'You're as ugly as sin; your breath stinks. No decent man could come with you, you disease-ridden prostitute.' He mashed the back of his hand across her face. Her scream was cut short, as he brought his head down with a crash on the bridge of her nose and she lost consciousness.

Coming to, slowly and painfully, in St James' Hospital, she remembered what had happened. A police woman filled in the details. She had been found in the laneway the morning after the attack, badly bruised, having lost a lot of blood, and near to death from exposure. She had needed surgery to her uterus; they set her broken nose, but the bone was badly shattered, and when eventually she got to see herself in the mirror, she was deeply shocked. The flesh around her eyes had ballooned into black car tubes, but she had seen herself like that before; she would recover from some of that disfigurement. It was her nose she could not believe! Deeply creased halfway down, it was purple, bent and flattened out over her cheeks. A Pekinese dog came to mind as she stared in horror at her new image. She would look better when the swelling had gone, they assured her, but she knew that her good looks were gone forever, lost as irretrievably as her innocence and trust in humanity.

She had lain in the hospital unconscious for three days. There was nothing by which to identify her except grotesque body art, branding her as Dommo's property. Nobody had reported a missing person answering her description. They had no idea who she was and it was best kept that way, she thought. The hospital was not sedating her half enough and she felt sick, sore and depressed. Knowing what she needed urgently, she stole clothes and snuck out of St James'.

She had returned to work the night after leaving the hospital, but in those past five weeks business had not been the same. Now, even in the aftermath of a good turn-on, she was a nervous wreck, hating every minute and in constant fear for her life. Winter had arrived, and she stood for long intervals between customers with the icy wind penetrating her flimsy clothing. For several hours each night there were veritable traffic jams along the canal, but now men inspected her from the warmth of their cars and drove past to invest in other goods. Often a much older woman plucked the prize from under Mags' broken nose.

Now her main customers were the sickos, and the men who wouldn't wear a condom, whom the other women wouldn't cater for. Luckily for Mags, this group were numerous. She had made several half-hearted attempts to use rubbers in the early days but between the bother and expense of buying them, the extra time and hassle of putting them on and the guys who refused to wear them anyway, she gave it up as a bad job.

Thoughts of becoming pregnant or of getting the virus seldom entered her head. She had long since stopped worrying about the discharges, even though some of what came from her body was foul and rank. The future was beyond her comprehension. Mags lived from fix to fix. The work dictated the need for the drug, the drug dictated the need for the work. This self-perpetuating cycle was her complete world.

The days of herself and Dommo doing snatches were over. Their dishevelled state alerted people to the danger and their lack of health made fight or flight impossible, so, accompanied by fear and terror, she dragged herself to the canal every night.

Nowadays it took her all her strength and will-power to get her up the stairs to the flat, but that was where the syringe was. She went into the room and threw the package onto the bed beside Dommo, who pounced on it and tore it open like a ravenous dog.

'Dat all?'

'Don't fuckin'well start now, you! That cost a hundred and twenty poxy quid. That's a lot a poxy customers.'

'I suppose there's fierce competition on the canal these days.'

'What are you tryin' to say? Wha'?' she shouted with such venom that Dommo jumped, spilling some of the drug.

'Jasus, Mags, love,' he said summoning up his meagre reserves of tolerance, 'I wasn't sayin' nuttin'. Was only tryin' to be nice, honest love.'

'Well I nearly froze to death. The wind pisses down that bleedin' river, an' if ya think I can work longer hours, ya have another thing comin', so ya have.'

Dommo knew that he had to have a fix fast or he would lose the head altogether and beat the hell out of her. Somehow he managed to be nice. 'Me poor darlin',' he said, taking her in his wasted arms. 'You're all upset. I'm sorry, I didn't mean nuttin', honest!'

'I'm not complainin', Dommo love,' she said, returning his hug. 'It's just that they're all gettin' it free nowadays. The priests used to be the big payers an' they're lying low since alla that shit on the telly about the bishop an' the American wan. The only tricks now are kinky bastards; you'd want to be a cross between an octopus an' a contortionist, tellin' ya. An' they expect it for nuttin' ... dirty mean bastards in their Mercs.' She was trying desperately to convince herself more so than Dommo.

'Snap outa it Mags, for fuck's sake.'

'Wha'?'

'Stop rabbitin', an' hurry in the name a Jasus!'

'Yea, ri'. Here give's it, I'll cook it up.'

'Will ya do the business for me?'

'Course.' As if he needed to ask, she thought. Did he think she was blind, or wha'? An' him shakin' so much he couldn't stand, let alone cook up the drug. 'I'm doin' me own first but!'

He wanted to object but thought the better of it. She prepared everything quickly and efficiently, injecting herself behind the knee after forcing a feeble vein to appear. Half the narcotic that she could afford to buy after her long night's work was not enough for a great turn-on, but it was enough

139

to make her feel human again.

It was enough so that she could cope with the smell of stale sweat and shit when she knelt down in front of Dommo and took down his trousers ... enough so that she did not retch at the sight of his scabby groin and penis. Enough for her not to vomit at the sight of the oozing sores around the tops of his legs. Enough so that she could put the spike into the big angry abscess beside his scrotum and draw out from each a syringeful of thick green, snot-like fluid, before she expressed it into the sink, refilled the scum-stained barrel with heroin and injected it into the perforated artery.

It was enough so that they could sit down together afterwards and discuss their future.

'Listen, Dommo, what's the buzz with this big job yav been rabbitin' about inanyway? It's not dangerous, is it? I won't have ya do antin' dangerous. Ja hear me now?'

'It's a cinch, an absolute beaut, not dicey arall. Listen, I'll put ya wide, provided ya tell no one. Ri'?'

'Course not!'

'Ri', see, all I have to do is ta take a little trip for meself to Holyhead, on the ferry like, an' bring back a case. Ya wide? Nuttin' could be easier, an' ja know how much of the awl spondulicks I get for that? Fifty grand, that's wha! For one poxy trip. I've a contact over there what I met inside. I just make a phone call to say when the pick-up is, and that's it. One poxy little trip an' no more problems, no more Garry, or any of the others on our back, no more canal. We could rent a decent gaff. I know this guy who opened a restaurant in town on the takin's from one bleedin' trip. Charges the yuppies fifty pound a head for a dinner. Fuckin' robbery if ya ask me.'

'Ya, what about the customs but?'

'Have that all covered, so I have. No bother arall.'

'Sure ya have.'

'Listen, customs is lookin' out for suitcases with false bottoms, cars with extra roof paddin', an' that like. But brainbox here will swan on through. Tellin' ya. Hold on a minute there, I wanna show ya some stuff I got.'

Dommo lay on the floor and propelled himself under the bed. 'Ri'. Shut your eyes,' he gasped, his voice muffled, 'an' don't open them till I tell ya.' Mags shut her eyes, and fantasised about what she would do with fifty thousand pounds.

She would buy a little house near her ma's place. But even before that, she would sign on for one a them de-tox programmes. She would get off the gear painlessly. She would take Tracy and her mother to Butlins for a holiday. No fuck it! They would have the best: they'd go to Disneyland.

Dommo would de-tox as well, an' they'd be as happy as antin' together in their little gaff. No more standin' around in the pissin' rain hoping that some fucker would stop for ya, an' at the same time prayin' that they wouldn't. No more pretendin' to be havin' a good time while they poked an' pulled at ya, an' all ya really wanted to do was puke. No more running on the ever accelerating treadmill of earning and yearning, of using and abusing.

'Ri', open them.'

She could hardly believe her eyes. An American tourist stood in front of her. Clad in an American baseball jacket with 'Berkeley' written across the front, Dommo was hardly recognisable.

Her turn-on was having a weird effect. She had this really strong sensation that Dommo did not exist, that he was nothing, a mere collection of ideas or sensations in her head which would melt into nothingness if she closed her eyes. It must have been the drug and his dressing up in strange clothes, but for a while she was sure that the whole world was just a figment of her imagination, that nothing really existed beyond her perception of it. She had to kick her toes off the wall to convince herself that there was some substance in the world.

He was wearing baseball boots and cap. There was a passport pouch on a leather string around his neck, and a huge red rucksack on his back.

'Hi, you guys. What ya reckon?' he drawled in what Mags

141

took to be a realistic American accent.

Christ, maybe her dreams could come true! 'Not fucking bad, partner,' she answered in such a bad attempt at an American accent that they both broke into laughter.

God, it felt so good to laugh! It relaxed her. She couldn't remember the last time she had had a giggle.

Striding bow-legged towards her, hands ready to draw six-shooters, Dommo took her in his arms and, chuckling, gave her a big hug. Jasus, what would she do without her fella? She returned the hug with all the puny strength of her track-marked arms.

'Does the gear go into the rucksack, Dommo?'

'Not arall! It's taped to ya back. It's only a couple a inches thick an' they'd never notice it, even with the rucksack off. They never stop any a them fuckin' students inanyway.'

'If they frisked ya but, Dommo, ya'd be in the shit.'

'They never frisk your back, an' cos it's on ya, it doesn't go through the place where the sniffer dogs do be. If the gear is in the baggage, it's poxy hard ta get it past the dogs. They get them hounds hooked on the gear, an' then withdraw it fast, make them go cold turkey. After that they only give them a fix if they sniff it outa someone's bag. Tellin' ya, it's cruelty ta animals. Course it's easier for a bird like.'

'What ja mean? How's it easier?'

'Like women can take it inside themselves. Ya wide?'

'Ya mean up them?' From her time in prison, Mags was familiar with these details, but they still disgusted her.

'An' down them as well.'

'How?'

'For fuck's sake! Ya tick or wha'? What they can't get up, they eat. They put it into rubbers, an' they coat them in jam so as they can swally them. Then they just walk through customs without a bother on them. Impossible to catch them!'

'Yea. How do they get it back but? What they swally like?'

'Some of it ya can puke up if ya stick ya fingers down ya neck, the rest ya just shit. Ya crap in the shower, it's easier ta make sure ya lose none an' ya can clean the rubbers that way.

142

Ya can get loads up ya but. That's what's great about it: a bird doesn't have to swally much arall.'

Dommo sounded matter of fact, but Mags looked perplexed.

'Would ya not shit yourself with nerves goin' through customs but?'

'No way. Ya just swally a fistful of valium about an hour before. That way ya sail through without a care in the world.'

Tracy had been whimpering for some time, and when Mags could no longer ignore her, she went to pick her up. Dommo stopped her.

'Leave her to me, love. I'll look after things. You take a rest.'

She was thrilled to get a chance to sit back and mellow out. The heroin she had bought tonight was good, and she felt relaxed. She watched as Dommo plastered pink cream over the baby's sores and put on a new nappy. He was great with Tracy, Mags thought. She was really lucky like that. When she was out working, he didn't neglect the baby like other blokes would. As long as he had his fix, he was happy to stay at home and play with her.

'We're nearly outa milk, Mags. Ja know what it is? Ya should a given her the tit. That way ya'd a saved me a lot a runnin' up and down them bleedin' stairs.'

'Don't be dirty, you! Inanyway, it's bad enough half a the awl fellas in Dublin hangin' out a them without her hangin' out a them as well!'

Having prepared the bottle, Dommo sat on the couch beside Mags and fed the child. She watched them closely as the baby's worried-old-man expression changed to one of contentment. But Dommo was looking poxy, Mags thought. He'd got really skinny, his bulging muscles were gone and his complexion was grey with blotchy red patches. It was all the worry. Garry and some of the other dealers from whom they had been buying lately, were getting heavy, calling around and making threats. She snuggled up to Dommo and put an arm around his skinny shoulders.

'Dommo, love.'

'Yes, pet?'

'I've been thinkin', so I have. The trip's too dangerous for you, what with your record, an' the cops on ya back an' alla that. I'll go.'

'Ah no, Mags! Ah Jasus, I couldn't let ya do that, love. No way!'

If my hypothesis is correct, that is, that the hidden agenda, the subtext of *The Rasherhouse,* is an attack on our prison system, an attack that is inspired by my critics in the feminist movement, then it is important for the intelligent reader to have an understanding of the nature and purpose of law. A comprehension of crime, the criminal and the criminal law must rest on such an understanding.

The law is used to protect ownership, to define the boundaries of private and public property, to regulate business, to raise revenue, and to provide compensation when agreements break down. Laws define the nature of institutions such as the family. Laws regulate marriage and divorce, the handling of dependent and neglected children and the inheritance of property. Laws also protect the legal and political system and establish who is subordinate to whom in a given situation. They maintain the status quo while permitting flexibility in times of change. Criminal laws protect private and public interests and preserve order. Society determines that some interests are so important that a formal system of control is necessary to preserve them; therefore laws must be passed to give the state the power of enforcement. Law thus becomes a formal system of social control that may be exercised when other forms of control are not effective.

Law may come from statutes and be known as statutory law, or from court decisions and be known as case law. Scholars, however, have argued over the historical source of law, some maintaining that such laws, deriving from rulers and referred to as 'positive' law, are not the only laws. 'Natural' law, it is argued, comes from a source higher than the rulers; it is referred to as 'higher' law, and is understood to be binding on people, even in the absence of, or when in conflict with, the laws of the sovereign power.

The concept of natural law can be found in the first known written legal document, the Code of Hammurabi, dating from about 1900 BC. This code was the embodiment of the existing rules and customs of Babylonia. The code incorporated the religious habits of the people and emphasised the importance of religious beliefs. It regulated pricing and marketing arrangements for goods. The 'an eye for an eye and a tooth for a tooth' philosophy was an integral part of the code. If a doctor performed a bad operation, his hand would be removed; if he was responsible for the death of a woman through miscarriage, the life of one of his daughters would be taken. Importantly, the code saw people's rights as being derived from supernatural forces, rather than from the monarch.

At the Nuremberg trials after World War II, the defendants rightly argued that they had broken no laws of the state. They had obeyed the orders they had got, which were based on those laws. The court accepted this as accurate, but nevertheless found the Nazis guilty. In other words, they were found guilty of breaking the natural law. They should have known that the God-given laws of nature always override man-made laws. These trials proved that there are two types of law, just and unjust, and since there is a moral obligation to obey just laws, there is also a moral obligation to disobey unjust laws. For a law to be just, it must be in accordance with God's moral law. Any law that promotes human dignity is just, while any law that degrades human dignity is unjust.

Nelson Mandela appealed to natural law; that is, he disobeyed certain laws on the basis that they were unjust and therefore that there was a moral requirement that they be challenged. In Ireland, because a small minority are forcing the laws further from God's moral law, in matters of sexual morality, for example, the right, in fact the requirement, for God-fearing people to disobey and challenge these laws grows each day. I found myself fighting a rearguard battle against those who were attempting to influence the law with the express intention of making it diverge from God's moral law.

'We have an old friend of yours, Paddy,' Prison Officer Rice shouted down the landing. Handcuffed to her was a pale and emaciated Mags. It was a while now since the police had let her have a fix from the heroin she had been caught with. In return for the drug, she had admitted everything. There was no point in trying to deny it. The heroin was strapped to her back, lodged in her vagina, and in her stomach. Keeping her in the police station, they had eventually retrieved everything, but she had not grassed. Nothing would induce her to name Dommo or the contact in Holyhead.

Ten years inside if she did not name names; out in twelve months if she did. That was the deal they had offered her. More tempting was the heroin they dangled in front of her broken nose. A good fix immediately and out on bail until the trial, with enough drugs to keep her going for a month. She was in the horrors, but Mags was no grass. She was in such a bad state that eventually they had given her sufficient heroin to keep her together long enough to sign the statement of her guilt and get her through the remand hearing. The judge had remanded her without bail.

As she was being led back into prison, she was finding it hard to keep her eyes open, yet at some deep level she was fully aware of what was happening.

She was aware she was back in the stark concrete and steel cage that was the women's prison. Back to the razor-wire nest of misogyny, the machine for the manufacture of stress beyond endurance and frustration beyond tolerance, with its psycho-toxic atmosphere. Back in the apparatus for grinding strong women weak and loving women hateful.

146

Paddy watched as the prisoner was led down the landing. Not until he took the paper from Rice and read the name did he realise who it was. A look of hopelessness transformed his country-red face. 'Margaret, you poor girleen. You look like you've been throught the mill. Are you all right?'

Mags' sharp but hopelessly confused senses smelt whiskey from his breath. 'Don't love me, ya alcoholic awl poxbottle.'

'We can put you back in with your old friend Betty, if you like, Margaret,' he said, ignoring her aggression.

'Oh no we can't!' Rice snapped.

'Yes! Fuck you and your "no"!' Mags was equally emphatic.

'Now, Margaret, let's not get off to a bad start this time. It looks as if we'll be spending an awful lot of time together in the future. Let's all co-operate and make life as easy as possible for one another, shall we?'

'There's nowhere else to put her.' Paddy's bushy eyebrows arched and he gestured helplessly with his hands. Rice tugged the handcuffs and towed Mags to her old cell. Paddy opened the cell and, as the cuffs were taken off, Mags slumped in and the door slammed shut behind her.

It was as if she had never been out, except that the Bible was thinner. Nothing had changed, the three bunks, the puke-green walls, the smelly pisspots.

Betty was in her usual bunk. Turning her head slowly, she looked at the newcomer with tired disinterest. 'Welcome to The Rasherhouse,' she mumbled, and turned, grumbling, back to the wall.

Even in her drugged state, Mags was shocked to discover that Betty had changed into a skinny, grey-haired old woman, with wrinkly skin which matched the green walls. Mags realised that she herself had degenerated, too, in the five months that she had been 'free'.

'Betty, it's me! Ja not recognise me? It's me, Mags!'

Bettty turned back form the wall and stared in confusion before a spark of recognition brought a fleeting moment of life to her eyes. 'Jasus! Mags me awl flower,' she drawled, trying hard to convey enthusiasm. 'Howya?'

'Howya, Betty?'

Both women hesitated, not knowing what to say. Eventually Mags carried on, unable to disguise the shock in her voice.

'You're lookin' a bit gammy, Betty. They treatin ya all ri' in here?'

'I've a bit of an awl flu, love, that's all. You're not lookin' the best yourself, so you're not. You're strung out ta fuck. What's the story? What they get ya for?'

'Importin'. Street value a million pound, they say.'

'Jasus! Ya pleadin' guilty, or wha'?'

'Guilty but insane!' Neither of them laughed.

Betty's eyes came to life. 'Ja bring antin' in with ya, Mags?' She held her breath, like a child waiting to see what was coming out of a favourite granny's pocket.

'Nuttin',' Mags said. Betty exhaled noisily. 'I've nuttin', Betty.' She broke down in tears. 'Scumbags say I'll get ten year.'

'Don't mind them, love, they're only windin' ya up, so they are.' Betty pulled Mags down onto the bunk and put her bony arm around her. 'Five, at the very most, Mags, an' ya'll be out in four.'

'Ja really believe that?'

'Swear on me mother's grave, Mags love.'

'Tracy'll be five be then!'

'Who put ya up to it anyhow? Was it that stupa bollix, Dommo?'

'Ah, Betty don't. It wasn't his fault. He didn't want me to go arall. An' he's lookin' after Tracy an' all. He's great with the kid, so he is. I don't know what I'd do without him, Betty, honest. I'd go outa me fuckin' tree altogether if it wasn't for Dommo.'

'Sure, Mags!' Betty said in a guarded tone.

'How long ja have that cold, Betty? Ya on a diet or wha'?'

'How could ya not be with the food in this kip?'

'Ya seen the doctor?'

'Leave it out, Mags, will ya?'

'What's the supply situation like nowadays, Betty?'

'Shitloads. They're not sharin' but. Most of it's up there with those toerags.' With tired eyes, she indicated the landing above. 'They're not dealin'. Must think I won't be able to pay back, so they must. I owe a good bit already, like, but I can make enough in a month on the canal ta pay back six months' supply, so I can.'

Metal rasped and the door was pushed open by Officer Kavanagh. 'Slop .... God, you again!' She too seemed to have aged by a decade in the last few months. Smile lines had been distorted into scowl markings.

'Yea, me! Missed ya beautiful face, so I did.'

'Well I can see that your attitude has not changed, whatever about anything else.' The young officer went to move to the next cell.

'Come 'ere. Tell the medic I need a de-tox, ri'? An' don't forget. I need it now. Ja hear me?'

'I hear you, Margaret. Not that you have to tell me; it's perfectly obvious. She will be on the landing in a minute, and she'll have your Phyceptone for you, don't you worry.'

Betty struggled to raise herself off the bunk.

'You stay there, Betty. I'll get your grub for ya.'

'Don't want any!'

'Ya have ta eat sometin'.'

'Leave it out, Mags. I don't want any.'

'Ri'. Sure I'm the very same. Couldn't give a shit if I never ate again. Goin' for me Phy but.'

Leaving the cell to find the medical officer and get her heroin substitute, Mags passed Officer Rice stepping into the cell.

'Come along, Betty, you must get up for your food.'

'Leave it out! Ya know I don't wanna.'

'But you must eat or you'll never get better. Look, you stay here and I'll get it for you.'

'Don't bother.'

'Listen to me, Betty; I shouldn't be telling you this because there is nothing official yet, but both the doctor and I have been speaking to the governor about you and we have recommended that your release date be brought forward.' She waited for some response but got none. 'I'm delighted to be able to say that he was in agreement.'

Lying on her back, Betty continued to stare at the bunk springs above.

'Do you understand what I'm saying to you, Betty? I'm telling you that you are going home shortly! In the next couple of days maybe!' Silence again. 'The department have only to give it their approval and you're out! Of course,' she said, switching back to a haughty official tone, 'it's not definite.' Unable to keep up the pretence of indifference, she continued in exasperation. 'But because the governor is giving it his recommendation, it's almost certain. Are you listening to me at all, Betty? Isn't it mighty news altogether?'

Betty fixed her with tired eyes. 'Ya mean,' she drawled, 'the kip is overcrowded an' ya have to fuck someone out to make room? Great! Thanks a bleedin' million.'

Shouting and screaming became audible over the usual chaos on the landing. Officer Rice shouted over her shoulder as she hurried out of the cell, 'Christ almighty, but there's no pleasing some people!'

She was back in the cell within seconds, gripping Mags by one arm, as Officer Kavanagh held the struggling prisoner by the other. They slammed the door shut.

'Fuckin' cunts,' Mags screamed at the closed door. 'That's not enough arall, an yis know it, so yis do, ya shower a fuckin' scumbags.' She turned to Betty. 'Would ya lukka all they gave me, in the name a Jasus!' she pleaded, holding up a plastic mug and indicating the level of Phyceptone. 'Sure I was on shitloads a gear. I can't survive on that bit. Sure any fuckin' eejit would know that!'

'Cool it, Mags, stop the shoutin'; you're wreckin' me head, so ya are. Inanyway, love, that should do ya for the night. It's not great like, but it's enough to get ya through till mornin'.'

150

Mags was crying again. 'For fuck's sake, Betty, that's not enough for me, not ta start with.' She drank the thick liquid, then cleaned the inside of the cup repeatedly with a shaking finger which she sucked to get every last particle. Within minutes she was calm. 'I'll have ta get to see the doctor tomorra, get her ta tell them to give me more. Nobody could go clean that quick. Meantime,' she jerked a finger towards the ceiling, 'I'll organise some gear from them fuckers upstairs. Dommo'll get me in enough ta pay back an' keep me goin', so's the Phy will just be a top-up, once I get organised.'

'Smashin', Mags. Will ya get them ta give ya enough for some for me? I didn't have a fix for weeks.'

'Course! Sure amn't I tellin' ya: Dommo will organise things for me soon. He wouldn't let me do years in this hell hole without keepin' me in supplies.'

'An' com'ere till I tell ya, Mags, I'll be out meself in a few days, an' I'll make sure ta get ya in a good bit.'

'Wha'? Out in a few days?'

'In a couple a days, they toll me.'

'Jasus, that's brillo, Betty. Ya sure but?'

'Yea! How many times do I have ta bleedin' well tell ya? They toll me. Ri'?'

'Betty, I'm delighra for ya, so I am. Here, that calls for a celebration. I'll organise a deal from upstairs. We'll have a party.'

'That would be smashin', Mags. Ja know what it is but?' she asked, the animation draining from her. 'I'm not sure they'll give ya any. They stopped supplyin' me after you left. Was in the horrors for weeks. Thought I was gonna die. Not jokin' ya.' Betty told her story all wrinkled brow and pleading eyes, like a little girl looking for sympathy from her mother. Mags put her arms around her.

'Listen, Betty love, I'll get us some gear, no sweat. I'm Dommo's bird and Dommo has friends up there.'

Mags went through the old routine, tapping on the pipes and checking the door.

'Who has gear these days?'

151

'Slug, I'm nearly certain.'

'Ay, Slug,' Mags yelled from the bunk top through the usual cacophony of window exchanges. 'Get up on ya springs, will ya, love?'

Through the tangled web of communications, a disinterested voice asked, 'Who the fuck's that?'

'It's me, Mags!'

'Back in wha'? What ja want?'

'Member all the fun you an' me an' Dommo had when we were in before?' she shouted slowly, giving each word significance. 'Member all the good times we shared?'

'Yea. Times is hard but. Ya know what I mean?'

'Listen, Slug, ya owe me one. Ya hearin' me? The least ya can do is to pay back a little now that I need ya. Listen, I'm Dommo's woman; ya know he has connections. Now alls I'm askin' is for ya ta pay back a favour. After that, he'll supply me direct.'

'I would if I fuckin'well could, Mags. I can't but. Ask anyone. I'm not windin' ya up.'

It was impossible to decipher nuances, but Mags reckoned that he wasn't lying. He sounded worried.

Letting go of the bars, she put her head in her hands wondering how she would get through the night on the amount of Phyceptone the medic had given her. Black thoughts were interrupted by Slug, shouting over the other voices.

'That's the last bleedin' thing I have, Mags, honest!' He sounded nervous. 'Hurry it up but.'

Mags' head shot up. Swinging past the window was the plastic bag. Grabbing it, she tore it open and discovered the same old syringe which had been on the rounds when she was last inside. It looked even worse for wear. Two big bullet-like tablets accompanied it. She held them up to Betty.

'What the fuck's them?' Mags asked.

'Two Nap hundreds.'

'It's not heroin, isn't it not?'

'No way, Mags. Morphine-based. It's better than nuttin''

but. Gives ya a bit of a buzz. We'll put them all inta the works together, instead a makin' two outa it. That way we won't lose any, an' we'll take half each outa it, ri'?'

Crumbling the tablets, they cooked the chalky substance as if it was heroin. When the fix was ready, Betty took the rusty old razor blade in her shaky hand.

'Haven't been able ta get a vein for ages, so I haven't. Have ta open one.'

Calmed by the Phyceptone and hardened by months of injecting herself and Dommo, Mags still found it hard to watch her old friend trying to cut open a vein on the back of her hand. Betty sliced into the bruised and wrinkled flesh several times without any sign of blood. With each cut she released a shrill cry of pain. Eventually, with the hand lacerated, Mags grabbed the blunt instrument.

'Here, gimme it for fuck's sake.'

Holding Betty's hand firmly, she made one deep incision into the grey, anaemic flesh, and a lazy drop of blood appeared in the wound. Taking the grimy syringe, she inserted the needle into the wound and up into the wasted vein. She forced the stopper halfway up the barrel, shooting chunky bits of chalk into Betty's sluggish bloodstream. Having withdrawn the needle, she wiped the blood off on a blanket.

Applying a tourniquet to the top of her own leg, she handed the works to Betty, turned around and leaned against the bunk.

'Squeeze a bit more,' Betty said, peering at the back of her leg. 'I can't find a vein for ya.'

Mags squeezed with all her might and eventually felt the prick of pain as Betty injected.

'Ya better start lookin' for another vein, Mags love, that one is just about fucked, so it is!'

Mags could not care less! She wasn't exactly buzzin' but she was floating nicely. Fuck worrying about tomorrow! She got the syringe back to Slug, and started stripping for bed.

'Will we have a little cuddle before we go to sleep?' Betty asked, her voice weaker than ever.

Mags looked at her sunken eyes and sweaty green pallor. 'Course, Betty love.'

Dreamily, she squeezed into the bunk beside her and Mags felt wanted and loved. As Betty's hands stroked the cheeks of her bottom and down the back of her thighs, a teasing tension mounted between Mags' legs and spread all over her hurt body. She dug her nails into Betty, desperately wanting release. Satin-soft fingers glided gently over her flesh. Butterfly wings brushed her and Mags' body exploded in wave after wave of body and mind-engulfing pleasure. Pent up tensions from months of ministering to the sexual needs of others gushed forth. As her pelvis jerked convulsively, she became aware of Betty whimpering with pleasure. They gasped for breath in unison, then kissed open-mouthed as their bodies went limp.

Thoughts of Dommo flashed through Mags' mind. Many's the night she had come home with the same needs and tensions but they had never had sex. Not that she could remember anyway, not really! A few times he had tried it with her, but it had been just like another customer torturing her abused body, to no avail for him and pain for her. He seemed to be going through an ownership ritual. Like the dominant baboon of the tribe, mounting her and thrusting several times before losing all interest. Occasionally, he ordered her to pull him off, and she went through the futile motions, before he fell into a comatose state, and she would cover his limp-pricked body with a blanket, wearily, to organise her own lonely release, if she could be bothered.

All thought of Dommo slipped from her mind as she drifted to sleep and dreamt she was lying on a feather bed in a warm pink room. This chamber was full of beautiful women, all radiant in their full-figured maturity. Naked except for fluffy towels wrapped around them, they were kind and sensitive. Each woman loved Mags and vied playfully with each other for opportunities to pamper her. She loved them all and felt secure in their company. They massaged her with scented oils and brushed her hair, while

154

discussing among themselves how beautiful she was. They were unanimous about her innocence and kindness. Gently, they lifted the soft covers and a woman got into bed on either side of her. Large soft breasts and smooth round hips secured her in a caress of loving tenderness, as she drifted to an enchanted sleep.

She awoke with a start. It was still dark, and the drugs had worn off. Her flesh was crawling with something. Scratching at herself until she drew blood made no difference. There were fleas all over her! No, it wasn't fleas, it was spiders! She could feel them crawling in her hair and trying to enter her mouth and ears. She punched at them with her fists, crushing them with blows to her body, but the more she killed, the more there were. The crawlies on her hair and around her eyes terrified her most. She pounded her fists on her head, but the spiders still attacked her relentlessly. Falling from the bunk, she crawled to the door and pounded it, screaming hysterically. They were eating her flesh away. She screeched and scratched and banged her head for hours.

After an age the door opened and a large black figure was framed in the blinding light.

'God almighty, what's come over you?' Officer Rice shouted.

'Get them offa me, get them offa me quick!' Mags screamed, scurrying, bruised and scratched, on all fours, out of the cell.

'Calm down this instant; there's nothing attacking you!'

Mags jumped to her feet and ran towards the shower. An officer went to stop her, but seeing the state she was in, let her be. With trembling hands Mags turned on the water, and as it gushed over her she calmed somewhat. She scrubbed her sore body. Time and again she lathered herself with the stinging soap until, exhausted, she sank down into a sitting position under the gushing showerhead.

'What on earth is wrong with you, Margaret?' Officer Rice was one of six officers standing around the shower.'Have you lost your reason?'

'I need more Phy!' Mags sobbed through the falling water. 'I toll ya I couldn't survive on the bit ya gave me. I need more, before I crack up altogether. Please?'

Her cadaverous, shaking body was streaked with long red scratch marks, and her face was contorted into an expression of horror. An officer turned the water off, stood Mags on her feet and helped her into a bathrobe.

'Come along now, Margaret, back to your cell. We've changed your blankets, so that you'll get a good night's sleep. You can see the doctor first thing in the morning.'

'No! Please don't send me back without more Phy, please?'

After a quick huddled council, a white-clad officer arrived and administered a dose of Phyceptone to Mags. She pleaded for more, but the medic insisted that it was enough to put an elephant to sleep.

Back in the cell, where Betty had slept on, each blanket was held up for Mags' inspection, to assure her that there were no spiders. Reluctantly, she let them put her to bed, where warming Phyceptone dragged her down to a sweaty sleep.

Mags hauled herself along with difficulty, each step like wading through treacle. She had no idea where she was going until she saw the canal, dark and drizzly. Through the fog, the big green man who had spied on her that first night leered at her with an evil grin.

She was frantically dragging herself away when a procession of cars appeared slowly and silently out of the fog. The first, a white Rolls Royce, was driven by an angelic man wearing a shining crown. Mags wanted him to pick her up and tried to flag him down, but the kindly driver smiled sadly at her and drove on by. The second car was blood-red and driven by a strong, arrogant man with a submachine gun slung over his shoulder. She wanted to hide from him, but he saw her, grinned contemptuously and drove on by. The third car was black, and the driver was calculating on a large computer as he drove. Seeing Mags, he entered some figure into the computer and drove on.

The fourth car was terrifying. It was so dirty and decrepit that she could not distinguish its colour. An air of doom hung about it. Its driver was deathly pale, and he fixed Mags with shrunken eyes from black sockets. Rats played on his shoulders and lice infested his putrid flesh. To Mags' anguish, this wreck stopped beside her, the door creaked open and she was drawn towards it. She tried to scream for help, but no sound would come. She was incapable of resisting.

Inside the car was a pestilent black cave, full of customers from her time on the canal. Each uglier than the next, all were partially dressed in filthy clothes, and panting with sexual arousal. The sickly smell of unwashed male genitals competed with the smells from their repulsive breath. An old man with furry-green teeth thrust his slug-like tongue deep into her mouth. Choking, she struggled in vain to push his foul body away. Hands pulled at her clothes, ripping and tearing them from her. Teeth bit into her breasts till blood flowed. Scabby pricks were driven into her every orifice until her mucus membrane was burnt and bleeding. Terror-stricken and racked with pain, she found her voice, and screeching, hammered on the door of the car.

The door opened and there stood Officer Rice.

'Christ almighty, what's all the screaming about now? Are you trying to waken the dead? Stop making an exhibition of yourself and get back to your bunk immediately.'

Finding herself in the cell, Mags experienced momentary relief. Too dazed and shocked to move, she stayed on all fours and stared up at the officer.

'We'll have to recommend the Central Mental Hospital for you, Margaret. You've really gone off the deep end this time.'

'I need more Phy,' Mags managed to whisper. 'Ask the medic ta get more Phy for me, please.'

'Come along with me Margaret.'

Mags struggled to her feet and stepped unsteadily onto the landing. The officer locked the cell, and helped her down the hall and into a narrow passageway. Opening a cell, she prodded the dazed prisoner in.

The door closed before Mags realised that she was in the black hole. Collapsing into the centre of the padded floor, she put her thumb into her mouth and curled up into the foetal position, a ball of physical and emotional pain. She craved drugs. More drugs, that's what she needed to get herself straightened out. Then she could come down slowly and never get into this mess again, ever. The stomach cramps were agonising, her intestines were ravaged by fire. Then she felt her bowels move, and she lay in the liquid shit in absolute misery.

She became aware that there were people in the pad. She was handled and moved, washed and dried. Eventually, she felt the heavenly glow of morphine flow through her veins as someone gave her an injection. She got the strength to stand and was walked back to her cell.

It was morning and Betty was sitting on her bunk dressed in her shabby tracksuit, a bulging Dunnes Stores plastic bag on her lap.

'Jasus, Mags, ya look in rag order, so ya do! Where were ya – the pad?'

'I think so.'

'What happened? I musta been out of it last night.'

'Last night?'

'Yea! Ja not remember? We had a Nap each an' a little cuddle, like. Ya know?'

'Jasus! I thought that was weeks ago. What's the story with the bag?'

'I'm gettin' out today,' Betty said, sounding sad.

Mags was devastated. Her only friend in the prison was leaving her, but buoyed up by the morphine, she tried her very best to seem pleased.

'Nice one, Betty! Jasus, that's only brillo. I'm thrilled for ya, so I am! Ya all excira?'

Betty broke down in tears.

'Aaaah, Jasus! What's wrong with ya, Betty?' Mags took her in her arms, fighting the impulse to cry herself. 'Ja not want ta go, or wha'?'

'Fuckin' sure I do! Ya mad?' Betty blew her nose in toilet paper. 'Still I'm kinda sad like, or sometin'.'

Both women laughed at Betty's confusion. Then, still in one another's arms, both cried. It was some minutes before they managed to recover enough to speak.

'Tell ya sometin', Mags. Now that I'm gettin' outa this kip, I'm never gonna score again, ever. Fuck heroin an alla that shit. I'm gonna kick the lot. An' as soon as I've paid back Rosie an' the others, I'll get meself a little flat an' make it nice an' cosy, big fire, telly, the lot. An' when you get outa here, there'll be a place for you an' the kid, if ya want. An' I'll get a decent job, so I will, no more workin' the canal or nuttin' like that, tellin' ya.'

Mags was unimpressed. She knew that Betty was fooling herself. She wanted to shake her, to shout at her to face up to reality. But what was reality? Was there such a thing, and if there was, would she recognise it herself?

She had just enough narcotic cradling her brain to keep her from yelling at Betty for her stupid delusion. Her senses were dulled enough to restrain her from throwing herself at her and begging her not to go and leave her to face years of hell alone.

It took the shock of Betty's release to make Mags realise that she loved her so much. She didn't want her to go back down the canal with her frail little body, fooling herself that it was only for a while. She wanted her to stay in the prison so that they could look after one another. Her eyes refilled but she struggled to hold back the tears.

'I can just see ya, Betty,' she managed to say, 'in your cosy little gaff. It'll be great.' The act failed her. Tears cascaded down, and she finished by crying out. 'I know it will, Betty love.'

Betty's tears flowed again in answer, as they sat with skinny tattooed arms wrapped around each other, swaying in grief. Betty desperately searched for something to say to console Mags. Eventually she managed to whisper. 'Listen, love, I'll come ta visit ya, an' I'll get ya in a little gear when I do. Don't you worry now, love, you'll be OK, so ya will.'

'Freedom awaits, Betty!' Officer Kavanagh boomed enthusiastically from the open cell door. 'This is the day you've been looking forward to. Come along now, there's a big world waiting for you out there.'

Betty disentangled from Mags and stood up, knowing that if she delayed, she might never find the strength to take her leave. She took her plastic bag and hobbled on weak legs out of the cell. Mags watched through flowing tears, as Betty headed down the landing. She looked so unsteady on her feet that the officer attempted to link her but Betty shrugged her off, straightened her back and quickened her pace.

Mags went to follow her, and watch her walk across the yard, towards the big grey gates to freedom, but Officer Rice blocked her way.

'Stay there, you. You have another six years to do, at least.' She guided the compliant prisoner into the cell just as the barred gate was opened for her departing friend.

Betty stood on the threshold, looking towards the gate to the outside world. She hesitated. The warm piss and disinfectant smell of the prison seemed to have woven a spell around her. She took a last look back. One cell, one landing, one exercise yard, her complete universe! A brutal dictatorship where rules and regulations replaced freedoms and choices. A society where the only points of reference were the daily battles of wits between the officers and prisoners, the struggle to overcome boredom, the quest for drugs, to beat the system and survive with some shred of dignity. This was all she knew now, after years of institutionalisation.

The prospect of the cold grey morning in the great unknown frightened her. She had longed for freedom, but now looking towards the gate, she shuddered at the prospect. A large hand pushed her gently and she went out and across the yard. Bored male eyes watched. Nobody bothered to shout. The landing gate shut behind her and the sound waves reverberated around Mags' brain, as she lay in her cell, knees pulled up, thumb in mouth.

Our author is here indicating that prison has not prepared the offender to re-enter society, that it has punished but not reformed. The reader is supposed to be shocked by this revelation. But what is prison but punishment, an attempt to redress the harm done to society, to make the offender pay for his or her wrong-doing? It is time to round off our education regarding crime and punishment, by looking at the history and development of laws. We shall see that since the beginnings of civilisation there has been a need for codes of behaviour in order that society could function and to minimise wrong-doing.

We have already discussed how, before the emergence of organised society, life was 'solitary, poor, nasty, brutish and short'. With the development of early forms of social organisation, informal controls emerged which were sufficient because of the simplicity of the society.

Every group has certain functions that must be performed in order that it can survive. Arrangements must be made for replacing members, providing food and other resources such as housing and clothing. It must be decided how much deviation from the norms of the group will be permitted, and what sanctions will be imposed on those who deviate.

As you know, when studying the 'ologies', particularly psychology and sociology, I advocate approach-ing them with a large pinch of salt. Full credit to the early sociologist, William Graham Summer, however, who in his book, *Folkways*, published in 1906, did sterling work in pointing to the importance of traditional behaviour and customs.

Summer pointed out that behaviour begins with acts, not thoughts. An act is a response to a need, and needs are satisfied by a trial and error method in an attempt to find the best solution. Gradually these ways of acting become routine. They are not creations of human purpose and wit, he says; they are the folkways and are the correct way of doing things because they are traditional. These folkways develop into doctrines of welfare, or as we call them mores.

In other words, folkways contain elements of what is

161

right and wrong, and when the distinction is extended to the public welfare, the result is mores – which tell people how to behave. They coerce and restrict the new generation without stimulating thought. Folkways make life easier and more predictable. They give discipline, and the support of habit and routine.

Codified law was unnecessary among primitive tribes because of the visibility of offences and the power of the community to deal with transgressors. Because there were few conflicting and competing interests, formal law was not needed to protect individuals' interests. Those who deviated from the norms of the group were easily spotted and the community could react with sanctions which were often more effective than laws. These sanctions might be a disapproving glance, an embarrassed silence, or social ostracism, with the threat of banishment from society being a very serious deterrent.

As more complex societies developed, however, a division of labour came about, and it became necessary to move beyond the informal methods of social control and to develop laws. Repressive sanctions were replaced with restitutive sanctions, which led to a more formal system of social control. As economies improved and a greater division of labour came about, there was an increasing rationality in general and in law. When people became capable of reflection and criticism, mores became laws, ending regulation by taboos.

Laws evolved from social interaction, reflecting the values of society and eventually becoming formalised. The laws could not, however, change the folkways and mores. Underlying the laws must be a consensus of values held by the people.

So we see clear historical evidence to support the consensus theory of the development and continuation of laws. Throughout the history of mankind, we see a slow but sure progression towards a more enlightened attitude to crime and punishment. Today's prison system is firmly based on respect for tradition, and reflects a high regard for the wisdom of the past generations, as they struggled towards the institutions of democracy which we now enjoy.

I will bring you back to the text, in the sure knowledge that now, having been introduced to the important issues in criminology, you will be able to interpret it in an informed and balanced manner. Being equipped to read the subtext critically, you will, from here on in, be aware of the writer's hidden agenda. You are now better educated about the issues than either the author or my critics, and as a result, I am confident that you will fully exonerate me of the failings of which they, in their ignorance, accused me. I take my leave of you, Dear Reader, for the last time, in the hope that you will in the future contribute to a more informed debate on these issues than has been possible up to now, and that in time you will form a bulwark of well-informed criticism of the type of harmful nonsense which is purveyed in *The Rasherhouse*.

As Paddy wished a bewildered Betty well at the main gate, Mags, in her new isolation, remained in the foetal position. The morning's fix was wearing off and the resulting discomforts were mounting towards pain. Turning on the bunk, she scratched herself violently wherever her nails could reach. She rolled off the mattress and began to pace the cell.

'Let me out, please God,' she shouted to the ceiling. 'I'll never do antin' wrong again, if only I get out to Dommo an' me little baby, pleeease! How could I stick this for years?'

Betty's departure was like a stab wound to her frayed nerves, which heightened her longing for Dommo and the child. She pounded the door.

'Let me out!' she shouted, 'let me outa here, please someone, please!' She put her hot forehead on the cool door, drew it back and smacked it off the metal. Her knees gave out, and she collapsed in a heap crying, as the door was wrenched open.

'In the name of Christ, look at the state of you again! Pull

163

yourself together, girl. What's all the fuss about this time?'

'I wanna see the psycho.'

'Look here, you! You're only back a wet day and you've caused havoc already. Just don't start making more demands.'

'I'm entitled to see the psycho, aren't I?'

'Oh you know your rights well enough! You're not too upset to know them, are you?' Rice's broad smile curled into a sneer. 'I'll put you on to his list. He should be in early next week.'

'Next bleedin' week?' The look of horror deepened on Mags' face. 'Well I wanna see the doctor then.'

'The doctor is not due in today. I'll put you on her list also. Now, have you any other requests? Is there anything else you would like done while I'm running around for you, Madam?'

'I'm entitled ta see the doctor any time I like, so I am, ya cunt ya."

'Don't you dare,' Rice hissed, closing the door with a back kick which locked them into the cell, 'don't you ever dare to call me those filthy names.' She advanced slowly towards Mags, swinging a large bunch of keys from a foot long chain. 'I'll soon sort you out, little missie!'

Mags scurried to the back wall and cowered in the corner like a beaten dog. 'No! No don't,' she pleaded, hands over her head. 'I'm sorry, I'm sorry. I didn't mean nuttin', honest! I just wanna see the doctor. I've a terrible pain in me head. I'll go mad if I don't get antin'. Please?'

'That doctor is too soft on you all. Ye have her wrapped around your little fingers, getting her to dole out drugs to you like they were Smarties.'

'I just need to talk to her. If I don't talk to someone, I'll kill meself, so I will!' The pleading whine gave way to sobbing. 'I'm not windin ya up, so I amn't.'

The officer put chain and keys back in her pocket. 'You addicts would do anything for a fix. God, it's pathetic!'

'I just need a bit more Phy ta get out of the horrors. I'll go on a programme an get offa the gear, honest, but I need sometin' just for now.'

'You can tell that to the doctor, but you don't fool me. I never saw one HIV positive addict break the habit, not one.'

'HIV? Who's HIV?' Mags wheezed as if the air had been punched out of her lungs. 'Are ya windin' me up, or wha'?' Her voice was rising. 'Are ya tryin' ta wreck me fuckin' head?' She was screaming now. 'Ya tryin' to drive me mad? Make me kill meself?'

'I'm sorry,' the officer stuttered, pale-faced. 'I thought you ... I mean, I assumed ... Look, I'm sorry.' She opened the door. 'I know nothing about these matters. I'm sorry I ever mentioned the virus. If you haven't got it, you haven't got it! I thought because –'

'Because ya want ta wreck me bleedin' head and drive me outa me fuckin' tree altogether, so ya do!'

Mags was on her feet again and walking towards the frightened officer, who went quickly out, slamming the door.

A wind-up, it had to be a fuckin' wind-up! Mags' head spun. How could they know? she wondered. She hadn't given a blood test, so they couldn't know. The rotten bastards, they were tryin' to drive her mad just for ta get their rocks off. That was it! No need to worry. Jasus! That time she was in the horrors in the padded cell and someone had given her a fix! Maybe they had taken a blood test then! She felt as if she was going to collapse. The very thought of dying slowly, painfully, and soon, in prison, without ever being free again! Maybe her withdrawal symptoms were so severe because she was beginning to die already!

Her legs turned to jelly, but she managed to collapse into a sitting position on the side of the bunk. She tried to figure it out. Could she have it? She did not use rubbers with the tricks. And the needles. Christ how many dirty needles had she used after other people? Hundreds! She was doing that before she had ever heard about the virus. Here in prison, where she had used her first needles, it was always after other users. There was no way of cleaning needles in prison, even if she had known what to do, which she didn't.

'Oh Mother of Divine Jasus!' she cried out to the heavens. 'I have AIDS! I'm dyin'!'

It was all so obvious to her now! Anyway, at the back of her mind, she had known that it was only a matter of time. But the thought of dying in a couple of years, when what you needed was a fix to get you out of the horrors did not seem important. A couple of years was an eternity to a junky, the future a fairy story for kids. What was real was the pain now!

Mags was only seventeen years old. Seventeen year-old people didn't die, she reasoned. They couldn't; they were only kids.

Christ, if it wasn't for Dommo she would want to end it now. Her head was pounding, she was sweating like a pig and stomach cramps scorched her intestines. Managing to get herself onto the pisspot, she shat smelly water as her stomach wretched and she tried to vomit at the same time.

She didn't even notice the door open, Rice take a fistful of her hair, pull her head back and empty a large measure of Phyceptone down her throat.

'That will keep you going for a while, Margaret.'

Within minutes she was calm. There was a taste of Phy in her mouth. She looked around the empty cell. Had someone given her a fix? If so, who, and where had the drug come from? Was it all a hallucination? Maybe this was all a terrible nightmare. Prison, the drugs, the virus, the canal, all the last months. Maybe she would wake up soon, at home with her baby in bed beside her.

Mags was exhausted but feeling better. The pains receded, as did the panic. She managed to stand and without pulling her clothes up, collapsed onto the bunk.

Sinking down through the mattress, weightless and worriless. A merciful veil of oblivion settled gently over her.

Plump and rosy-cheeked, Mags lay on a soft bed in a beautiful room. Around her, Dommo spoke to her mother while Betty, radiant and healthy, helped Tracy play with an array of expensive toys. They chatted happily among themselves. Mags felt weak but cheerful. Everyone knew she was dying of the virus and all were happily resigned to the fact.

Floating off the bed, she was already on her way up to heaven and looking forward to her arrival, but she was lonely at the prospect of leaving her family; the thought of parting from them spoiled her otherwise perfect state of mind. Sweet-tasting tears ran down her cheeks as she focused on her baby. The child put her arms up in an attempt to hold her down, but she was already beyond her reach. Tracy began to cry.

Mags was speechless in her profound loneliness.

She wanted to tell the child that it was all for the best, that she was going somewhere wonderful and in time they would be together again.

'Wake up, Mags,' her mother called out. The voice became strange and harsh. 'Wake up and get out of that bunk this instant, Margaret. You've been asleep for a whole day. Get up immediately and eat some breakfast.'

Her eyelids unglued painfully, revealing a blurred semi-circle of officers around her bunk, one of whom was shaking her violently. 'She should be all right now,' a strange voice said. 'Get her up and showered and make her eat something. And never give anyone, no matter how sick they are, that amount of Phyceptone again!'

Too weak to resist, Mags was marched down the landing to the shower, which revived her enough to make her aware of her misery.

'Will the doctor be in soon?'

'She should be in before eleven, Margaret. Don't worry, you're on the top of her list.'

'What time's it now?'

'Nearly ten.'

Slouching back to her cell, helped by an officer, she heard her name bellowed from the top of the landing.

'For the doctor?' she shouted back, wide-eyed with hope.

'Visit,' the voice roared back.

She was finding it hard to stay awake and on her feet, but she was not going to miss the chance of a visit from Dommo. Just in time, she thought. He'd have gear for her. She felt better already.

167

Officer Rice beckoned Officer Kavanagh to follow, and, handcuffing Mags to herself, led her down the landing.

At the visiting box, Mags was devastated to discover that Dommo was not there. It was only her mother and Tracy, yet immediately her deep running maternal instinct took over in a rush of love and longing for her child.

Her mother could not believe that this bent stick figure was her own daughter, who had been so beautiful and healthy a mere ten months before. She could not bear to look at her blotched face with its disfigured nose.

Kicking and trying to wriggle out of her grandmother's grip, Tracy held her little arms up in Mags' direction, gabbling word-like sounds. Mags ran towards the partition to take the baby in her arms. 'Tracy, me poor little –' She was jerked back abruptly by the handcuff on her wrist, but she dragged the officer to the partition and tried to take the baby.

'No physical contact, Margaret.'

'Wha' ya fuckin'well talkin' about?'

'No touching.'

'It's me baby,' she shouted, bursting into tears. 'I'm all she's got. I'm her mother.'

'You know the rules, Margaret.'

'I always held her before,' she sobbed, as Tracy's excitement turned to tears of frustration.

'Yes indeed! And there were always drugs in the prison before.'

'Me little baby isn't a drug pusher. Me Mammy isn't a drug pusher. They've never done nuttin' wrong.'

'Mags, love,' her mother managed to make herself heard above the shouting. 'Don't upset yourself, my little pet. You'll only make the baby worse. Be strong now, like a good girl. For your mother.'

'Gimme me baby,' Mags pleaded, collapsing onto the plastic seat.

'Calm down now and stop your nonsense.' Rice's tone was threatening.

'What did I ever do on you? You're deliberately windin'

me up, so ya are, tryin' ta drive me mad.'

'If you don't stop this childish nonsense right now, Margaret, I'll be forced to put an end to the visit.'

'Please don't upset yourself, Mags. The baby is just fine with me. She's only crying because she has wind or something. If we all quieten down, she'll be all right. This is the first time she's been upset since I got her.'

'What ja mean?' Mags demanded, snapping out of her tears. 'I thought Dommo was lookin' after her?'

Her mother's face went from palest grey to brightest red. 'He er ... he got a job, Mags. He couldn't work and look after her, so ... he ... er, left her with me. He misses her like mad, so he does, has me plagued comin' up to see her every chance he gets, like.'

Tracy calmed somewhat. Mags stared with pinhead-pupil eyes at her mother, who continued nervously, 'You're worried about the trial, aren't you, love? Well you're not ta. Sure the judge will know that it's help you need, not punishment. Ya won't get a long sentence; I just know you won't, love. And the time you do spend in here will do you the world of good. You'll be away from the drugs at least. And when you get out, you'll have the drugs out of your system and you'll be able to make a new start.'

Mags took in nothing of what her mother was saying. There were questions she wanted to ask about Dommo's 'job', but she couldn't with an officer on either side of her. She stared longingly at the baby. Only her deep fatigue stopped her from jumping across the partition to her child.

'They say the solicitor you've been given is very good,' her mother carried on. 'He'll tell the judge about your drug problem, Mags. He'll make sure ya don't have to spend long in here, love. Are they giving you the medication you need?'

The word 'medication' brought Mags' attention back to her mother. 'Not enough for a sparra! Ma, will ya ask ta see someone high up, an' get them ta let me see the psycho? Will ya, Ma? He'll know I need more medication. Not for ever! Just till I'm over the trial, like. I'll be better after that, I know I will,

169

an' I'll go clean then, honest I will, Ma.'

'Time up please.'

'I'll talk to anyone who can help ya, love, anyone. But you must be strong now, Mags. Things will work out, love. You're safe in here.'

'I'm sorry, but I have to end the visit now.'

Fighting back tears, Mags' mother stood, with the bewildered baby in her arms. The officer lifted Mags out of the chair and gently moved her towards the exit.

'I'll come an' visit ya tomorrow, Mags. Ya remember what day it is, don't ya?'

'Tomorra is a million year away, Ma.'

'Ah, Mags love!' She tried to chide her daughter cheerfully, failing miserably, 'Tomorrow is your eighteenth birthday, love. It's a big day in a young wan's life, so it is.' She struggled bravely through the tears. 'I'll bring ya in a cake, the type you like, an' we'll eat it here together, you, me an' Tracy. It will be nice, love. An' I'll have a little present for ya as well, so I will.' She took the baby's hand and waved it in Mags' direction. 'Wave bye bye to Mammy now, that's a good girl. Wave bye bye.'

Rice had managed to half-guide, half-carry Mags as far as the door of the visiting box. Officer Kavanagh stared at her colleague – both officers were pale-faced and red-eyed.

'Ma?'

'Yes, pet.'

'Will ya tell Dommo ta visit me as quick as he can? Will ya, Ma?'

'I will, love, but he's sorta busy and he might not be able to make it for a few days, pet.'

'Ma.'

'Yes pet?'

'I love you, Ma.'

'I love you too, pet.'

As Mags slouched out of the visiting box, her mother slumped into the chair, hugging the baby to herself as she cried.

Once outside, Rice took the cuffs off Mags and instructed Officer Kavanagh to take her back to the cell. The younger officer grabbed her superior by the arm. 'Could you not ...' she hissed, her voice laden with confused emotions. 'I mean, did you have to ...'

'Don't!' the older officer snapped viciously, wrenching the hand off her arm. 'Just don't you open your mouth! If you think that I enjoyed that scene any more that you did, you have another thing coming!' She pointed a shaking finger in the younger officer's face. 'When you're in charge, you can allow yourself the luxury of a more humanitarian regime in the visiting box and take the flak for the prison swimming in drugs, but while I'm here I'll do my best to keep them out, no matter what the cost, because in the long run it's the most humane thing to do! Now follow her, please, and keep her out of harm's way. If you don't mind, officer.'

Pale and shaking, Rice went back into the visiting box to Mags' mother.

'Can I get you a cup of tea, Mrs McGowan?'

'Is there nothing ye can do for her? She looks so sick and unhappy.'

'We're doing all we can for her, really we are. She's getting Phyceptone twice a day; she's to see the doctor later on, and she is on the psychologist's list also. You must understand she was on massive doses of heroin before she came in, so it will take time before she comes back to her full health. Are you sure I can't get you a cup of tea?'

'No thanks.' Mrs McGowan stood with difficulty and, carrying the baby, walked to the main gate.

Crossing the exercise yard on the way back from the visit, Mags never even heard the obscenities shouted from the windows above. Back on the landing, Kavanagh went ahead to open the cell door, and Mags bumped into Rosie.

'Jasus, Mags, ya look manky. Strung out, wha'?'

'Rosie, I need some gear, bad!'

'Sorry, love, I've nuttin' ta give ya.'

'Please, Rosie, I'm in a bad way.'

'I can see that, like I said, but I've nuttin'. Supply problems!'

'Dommo will make sure ya get paid for it. He'll pay ya antin' for it, antin'.'

'Will in his bollix.' Rosie swaggered off, a knowing smirk distorting her war paint.

Confused and distressed, Mags went into her cell and lay on the bunk. Somehow she got through the day. She was called by the doctor, who slightly increased her dosage of Phyceptone. Mags cried and pleaded for more, but the doctor was adamant that any more would do her harm. She struggled through nightmares, through ordeals beyond human endurance, as her emaciated body acted as a conductor for all the horror and ugliness in the world. When night fell, she dragged herself up on the springs and shouted through the bars and broken glass.

'Slug?'

'Who's that?'

'S'me, Mags.'

'Wha' ja want?'

'De awl message, Slug,' Mags shouted, finding it difficult because of her weakness to make herself heard. 'Ya wide, the stars an alla dat.'

'No joy. It's just another starless night.'

'Listen, Slug, ya have ta help. I need some gear, bad.'

'Shut ta fuck up, ya stupa cunt. Ya tryin' ta set me up or wha'?'

'No, Slug, listen. Dommo'll look after ya well. He'll see ya all ri', honest.'

'An' what about you? If I ask for a visit from ya, will you see me all ri', Mags, hah?'

Slug's voice had changed, now he was jocular and mischievous. Mags could only barely manage the energy to keep up the conversation, but it sounded more hopeful now, so a couple of seconds later her voice competed with the others shouting at the windows.

'Course, Slug, I'd see ya right.'

'Would ya give me the awl rub a the rasher?'

'Yea, Slug. What about the stars but?'

'Would ya give me an awl ride, Mags?'

'Yea.' Tears could be heard in her voice.

Having got the drift of Slug's line of questioning, the other prisoners at the windows quietened in expectation of a bit of craic.

'What ja say, Mags? I can't hear ya proper.'

'I said yea, Slug,' Mags shouted through her tears. 'I said I'd give ya a ride, Slug. What about the ...'

'Would ya give me a blow job, Mags?'

'Yes,' Mags cried bitterly. 'Yes.' Their conversation was now being punctuated by about twenty male voices, laughing, whooping and contributing their own obscene suggestions to the dialogue.

'Would ya eat me shit, Mags?' Slug continued, to howls of laughter.

'I'd do antin', Slug if ya'd just ...'

Slug had a good reputation as an entertainer. Knowing his style by now, the other windows fell silent.

'I said, Mags, would ya eat me shit?'

'Yea, yea, antin', antin'.'

'Ri'! Listen up to me good, Mags.' His voice echoed around the dark and empty yard. 'Ya can eat ya own fuckin' shit, Mags, so ya can, cos Dommo'll never settle up any more accounts for you, ya stupid cunt ya! He moved in with Winnie the day after you landed back in this kip. Ja think he'd hang round for ten year waitin' for an ugly puss like yours, well past its sell-by date?'

The listeners exploded in a riot of laughter.

Mags' head jerked back on her shoulders as if she had been kicked on the forehead. She half fell, half jumped off the bunk, and landing in a heap on the floor, stayed like that in stunned silence, as the hilarity continued. The laughter registered in her brain like the screaming of the devils of hell.

As the satanic cacophony swirled round her brain, she jumped to her feet. In a manic fury she pulled the mattresses off the bunks and smashed the pisspot against the wall; she kicked the press and the table.

Out on the landing, Officer Paddy thought he heard a noise from one of the cells and decided to check it out as soon as the new prisoner they were admitting was settled in. She was only a child really, and himself, Rice and Kavanagh, were having to put up with the usual insults and threats from her.

Frothing at the mouth, Mags upturned the bunks and smashed them on the ground. The Bible was flung against the door. She was stopped dead by a small tinkling noise which insinuated itself through the uproar in her head, as the rusty razor blade fell from the Bible cover. She stared at it motionless before picking it up.

Ripping off her teeshirt, she held the blade over the tattoo on her chest. With lightning speed she slashed the rusty blade across her flesh. Blood oozed from collar bone to nipple and, flowing slowly over 'I love Dommo', began dripping onto the blankets. The second slash was across her left wrist. Blood flowed fast from that wound. Neither cut had hurt more than mainlining with a blunt needle. She smiled, wondering why she had not done this long ago, so saving herself a lot of suffering.

She lay down on the pile of blankets and, leaving her bleeding arm out, wrapped them around herself. Energy flowed from her. It was quite a nice feeling really, a bit like goofing off on heroin. Yes, not a bad buzz at all! She began to float in the air without a care or worry. At peace.

A picture of her mother and Tracy, with arms stretched heavenwards and pleading eyes, came to Mags' failing mind. Suddenly, she felt more lonely than she had ever felt in her life. She couldn't drift off without them. Jesus Christ, what had she been thinking about?

Struggling to stand, she wrapped her teeshirt around her haemorrhaging wrist. Her strength failed her and she collapsed and crawled to the door to bang for help. She managed to give it one or two feeble knocks, but was too weak and exhausted to give it a decent thump. She would rest a while to get the energy to make herself heard. But she was afraid that she might go to sleep, afraid of the lonely void, terrified to face the ultimate trip alone. She would lie on the blankets for a while, just for a few seconds, until she had rested a bit.

Sadly, Seán Howard was called to his maker shortly after completing the work of criticising (or 'deconstructing' as he would have it) the above text, and since he never married, it fell to me, his close friend, to put his papers in order. Seán suffered from sclerosis of the liver, a painful and debilitating condition, yet it did not deter him from his work. His major concern, as he became more sick and feeble, was that this manuscript be published, and so vindicate his reputation as a prison reformer.

Throughout his life of dedication to the cause of prison reform, he had to endure the spectacle of mischievous authors furthering their dubious careers by publishing such filth. It was not only the pornographic nature of these works which upset him, it was the hidden agenda, the subtle subtext, which he felt was so dangerous for our society. But he has spoken eloquently to you of these matters, and I need not list the dangers which he saw accruing from such works.

During a brilliant career in the Department of Justice, Seán educated himself on all the issues about which he has written – crime, punishment, censorship, and the many theories which purport to explain the sad phenomenon of deviances in society, but his social commitment did not stop there. He was a deeply committed Christian and a respected member of Opus Dei, through which I had the pleasure of becoming his friend. One of the sweetest fruits of his work was the birth of the Christian Coalition Party, which he helped to found, thereby playing an important role in Irish political affairs. The party, which was in no small way his brainchild, lives on after him, to continue the struggle to stop Ireland's slide towards a secular state whose legislation no longer reflects the laws of God.

Because of Seán's involvement in politics, he became the target of the extreme wing of the feminist movement, and for several years he had to suffer silently the slings and arrows of their vitriolic abuse. His eventual early retirement was forced after a slanderous campaign against him, orchestrated by a few vengeful women. The rumours against Seán were, I have every confidence in saying, unfounded, but typical of a man of such strong principles, he felt he had to resign, even though the young woman who was at the centre of the controversy was infamously unreliable, if not downright unbalanced. How sad that one such hysterical and politically motivated woman could end the career of a great and dedicated man. But enforced early retirement could not crush Seán Howard's commitment to Christian values.

Spanning the decades from the 1960s to the 1990s, his career coincided with a period of great change and disturbance in Ireland, a period when our traditional Christian values were besieged and attacked on all fronts. It was a time when the forces of liberalism attempted to manipulate our people into an acceptance of divorce, contraception and abortion. It is to the eternal credit of the virtuous and committed few who could point to the danger of the theories, which attempted to dress up these moves and make them look acceptable, that our traditional values remain still largely intact. Central among this valiant group was Seán Howard.

The evil empire of communism having been all but crushed without having seriously polluted our shores, there still remains another, less obvious, but nonetheless dangerous, enemy within. I speak of liberal secularism. That the 1990s has seen the signs of a lifting of the siege of liberalism and a timid but notable reawakening of our traditional Christian values, owes more than a little to Seán, and to be remembered for this would, I'm sure, be his greatest wish fulfilled.

This book is published in memory of Seán Howard, scholar, gentleman, criminologist, man of letters and man of God. It was his wish that it introduce a new generation to the difficult and intractable theoretical issues behind the problems of prison reform.